ALSO BY LEIA STONE

MATED GIRL

LEIA STONE

Bloom books

To my beautiful children.

Published by Bloom Books, an imprint of Sourcebooks
1935 Brookdale RD, Naperville, IL 60563-2773
(630) 961-3900
sourcebooks.com

Originally self-published in 2021 by Leia Stone LLC.

Cataloging-in-Publication data is on file with the Library of Congress.

Printed and bound in the United States of America.
POD

CHAPTER ONE

AFTER TALKING TO MY MOM ABOUT DECIDING TO break Sawyer out of Magic City Prison, I slipped into the shower. The water ran down my body in warm rivulets and I sighed. I was glad that the Ithaki hadn't damaged the gravity-fed water tower when they'd ransacked Paladin Village. I'd missed this, showering with soap and shaving my legs, but I'd be lying if I said I didn't miss that little cabin in the woods and my time there.

My thoughts were a frantic tangle of how exactly I would get to Magic City Prison, which was in the middle of high-tech Light Fey City, and then how I would break Sawyer out. Sawyer had indicated that the vampires would be waiting for me to rescue him, which meant going there was a trap…but I had no way around that. I was a one-woman show, although I knew Sage would insist on going with me and I wouldn't have it any other way…but still. How did two women break into a magic prison? I had seven days to get him out before they killed him, and that was not enough time, especially considering I was basically a wanted woman with a target on my own back.

I forced down the sob that threatened to come back up. Now was not the time for a breakdown. Sawyer had seemed so hopeless when we'd last spoken. It broke my heart. I'd be hopeless too if I'd just been sentenced to death by guillotine.

I couldn't let that happen.

I was also worried about leaving Creek, but if you had to leave your baby with anyone for an extended period of time, it felt good when it was your own mother.

After turning off the tap and changing into fresh clothes, I slipped into the living room to find Eugene, Sage, and Rab all bent over a map of Magic City. They held steaming cups of tea and coffee and were speaking animatedly about something.

"What's going on here?" I asked, frowning at the food wrappers and old coffee cups that littered the table. "Have any of you slept?"

Sage looked like a zombie, hair in a messy bun, dark circles under her eyes, her left foot tapping out a rhythm like she'd had too much coffee.

She grinned as I approached, her eyes widening, which made her look even more amped up. "Eugene knows a guy who broke out of Magic City Prison a decade ago."

I froze, my heart picking up speed until it was a steady thump in my chest. "I...I need to see him. Who is it? I need him to tell me everything, I need—"

"He's a troll," Eugene said, putting up his hands. "Went into hiding years ago. Haven't spoken to him in a decade."

Damn!

I'd assumed a wolf friend, preferably one still alive and here in Paladin Village. I started to pace the room, my mind spinning as I chewed on this new information.

Rab stood, stepping in front of me. "We've been up all night. We've decided that we three will go and try to bring Sawyer back...while you stay and take care of the pack."

I looked at Rab with what I hoped was a grateful expression and not one of murder, which was what I was currently feeling. "That's really sweet, you guys, but I can't let you all do that. I have to be the one to go."

Sawyer was my damn husband, mate, and baby daddy. No one was going for him but me.

Rab shook his head. "You are the alpha, the most important—"

"What if it was Willow?" I stopped him. "Would you trust anyone else to get her back?"

He sighed, shrugging as a defeated expression crossed his face. "You can't go alone, and we can't leave the entire pack without leadership."

I nodded. "You, Eugene, and Star will lead the pack while Sage and I go. It's been the two of us forever. We can do this together."

I looked at my bestie as her face pinched, like she was fighting the urge to cry.

"I'm totally going, not even up for discussion," she added to Rab.

He growled lightly, running his fingers over the long scar on his face. "We just got an alpha, we are just starting to rebuild..."

I nodded. "And when I bring Sawyer back, we will build back stronger than ever before."

He sighed, giving me a curt nod. Then an idea struck me.

Troll.

The guy Eugene knew was a troll.

"Marmal!" I shouted, causing everyone to jump. "We can go see my troll friend Marmal. Maybe she can help us find this guy that Eugene knows!"

Eugene shrugged from his place on the couch, where he nursed a steaming hot mug. "The trolls are notorious for their gossip and stories. Maybe she's heard of him."

I'm sure she had. Marmal said people in Troll Village paid in gossip. If a fellow troll had escaped Magic City Prison, she would know the story and possibly where to find him.

"We'll leave right away!" I started to look around the room for what to bring.

"Hold up." Rab put his hands out. "Our people *just* settled here. They will want to see you first, to have faith in this new home you've brought them to."

I growled, not excited to play politics right now. But he was right. I'd need to make a small appearance before I left. "Fine. Sage, you get two horses ready. Pack them up with enough food for a week and I'll go make one round outside through the village. We leave in an hour for Troll Village."

I wasn't letting Sawyer die because I had to uphold some image.

Sage nodded and stepped toward me, pulling something from her pocket. "In all the drama, I forgot to give this back. Your mom held on to it for me when I went looking for you." She reached out her hand and my breath caught in my throat.

My ring.

I plucked it from her palm and slipped it on my ring finger. It felt so foreign to wear jewelry after a year in the wild, and yet this ring felt like home. It made me miss Sawyer so much more. "Thank you," I croaked.

Rab stepped outside, ushering me to do the same, and I nodded. Sage then handed me a cup of coffee and a breakfast burrito, which I took gratefully. My hair was still damp, but I stepped out into the chilly morning air and took in the sights of my people, of our new home.

The first thing I noticed were the smiles. People were laughing, drinking from steaming hot mugs that had been heated over campfires, as they breathed in fresh air. After living off the land for a year, I couldn't imagine hiding in a concrete bunker. Emotion clogged my throat when I noticed all of the fresh green grass, yellow and pink flowers, fern bushes. The land was still magically restoring itself, but it looked like it had become a garden wonderland overnight. Every tree was thick with leaves, every patch of ground covered in grass or moss, and each house still standing blanketed in creeping vines and flowers.

It was the physical manifestation of what I'd done in that cave by giving my magic to my people and this land, and it blew me away with pride and gratitude.

"The village has never looked more beautiful," Rab said, startling me from my thoughts. "I checked on the fields a few hours ago. The corn, avocados, peaches, barley, peas, it's all growing back at a rapid rate, with no sight of disease."

A tear slipped down my cheek as my throat tightened. This right here made it all worth it. The year away, not being there for Sawyer, it was a hard choice, but I'd saved thousands of Paladins, and now thousands of city wolves, as this land would be their safe haven until we could take Wolf City back.

I inhaled through my nose. Mixed with the flowers was the smell of magic, *my magic*, Paladin magic. This land was special, and I think even the city wolves sensed that. Trying to push Sawyer from my mind and the sense of urgency I felt to get to him and to Marmal to find this troll, I forced myself to calm down and take a breath, to enjoy this moment of what I had accomplished for our people.

"A lot of people want to thank you," Rab said. "Come on."

I followed him into the little campsites where people were waking up and sitting in front of fires as they made breakfast.

"Thank you, Alpha!" a Paladin woman with one kid on each hip called out to me as I passed. I gave her a small smile and nodded my head. People were out and about, stretching and looking up at the rising sun. Imagine a year underground and then coming back to this Garden of Eden.

"She healed our land!" another said, and I suddenly felt awkward with the public attention, but continued to walk and be seen like Rab said. I didn't want to be known as an absent leader, especially if I was going away for a while. I sipped my coffee and nibbled my burrito as I waved and nodded at people who we passed by.

We came upon an open field where a bunch of city wolves seemed to be surveying the land and pointing out different areas for building. I recognized one of them as the man who'd almost challenged me in the bunker. As if sensing me behind him, he turned. There was regret in his eyes, even shame. He gave me a small nod of his head and I nodded back. That was as much of an apology as I was going to get.

"Hey, I heard you're leaving soon," Willow called to me from behind. I turned to see her holding her daughter. The baby looked so much like her mother, all except for the beautiful brown eyes she had compared to her mother's Paladin blue. She would forever be known in our community as one of the few Paladin children born without wolf shifter magic in the time that we had no alpha...and I would hold guilt over that for the rest of my life.

Still, she was perfect.

I'd been worried Creek would be born without a wolf since he too was born before I'd claimed the land, but I could smell his wolf just under his skin, something he got from his father and my city wolf lineage no doubt. In that case, his wolf wouldn't emerge until around his first birthday, as was normal in city wolf genetics.

"Yeah, I'm just making the rounds," I told Willow, "and then I'm going to get Sawyer and bring him back."

She nodded as if she understood, and then booped her daughter's nose. "I'm taking Daisy for a playdate with Creek, and then I'm going to make mashed corn soup!" She said the last few words in an excited voice to the baby, who blew a raspberry in her face.

I smiled. Willow was such a natural mother, and I loved the name Daisy. In all the drama I'd totally forgotten to ask what they'd named her. I had a dark thought then. What if Sage, Sawyer, Walsh and I all died and none of us made it back? Who would take care of Creek?

My mom was great but she wasn't a warrior. What if the Ithaki attacked and she died too and there was no one to take care of my son? Panic seized me.

"Hey, Willow, Rab..." I looked at them both awkwardly, deciding something in the spur of the moment. They stared at me with concern, probably because I sounded on the verge of tears. "I, uh, my mom's going to be looking after Creek while I'm gone, but if something were to happen to her, and my dad... and I didn't come home..." I blew air through my lips nervously. "If anything happens to me, will you make sure Creek is taken care of?" My throat tightened with emotion at that thought, but it was a very real thing to have to think about right now. Sage and I were going on a dangerous mission and I *needed* to know my son would be okay.

Willow grabbed her heart, clutching Daisy closer to her as tears lined her eyes. As a new mother, I hoped she understood my panic.

"I hope that *never* happens, but if it does, that baby boy will have a long and happy life," Willow promised. "I'll make sure of it."

"Me too," Rab said. "We will provide for him and protect him with our lives, as if he were our own."

A huge weight lifted off of me then. That was what I needed to hear. Now I was ready to go fight for my man.

———•·•———

The horses that the Paladins kept on the back side of the land had grazed the wild grasses and drank from the stream over the past year, so they were in pretty good shape. Sage was able to convince two of them to wear a saddle, so we were in luck. It had been a year since either had been ridden, but they seemed okay with it, other than some twitchy tails. I couldn't go into Wolf City and get a car and just drive on over to Troll Village, so this was the next best thing. Saying goodbye to the Paladin Village this morning had been hard. Our two wolf packs were trying to start fresh, and I was supposed to be their leader and I was leaving. But I *had* to do this.

Because I was linked to this land, I knew our territory without even looking down for the blue stone crushed path. I felt it like a guideline just under my skin. Some parts felt and smelled like home and the others were foreign. Not that it mattered much since the Ithaki had broken the peace agreement and we were at war with everyone. But, luckily, it was a short trek through the Wild Lands on horseback and to the edge of Troll Village.

The problem was that Marmal's farm was at the very outer edge, near Vampire City, and we were going to have to come up through the entire village to find her. Once we stepped inside troll territory, it would be a full day's ride. I'd painted Sage's face with blue paint and dressed her to look like a Paladin trader. Wearing deer skin that barely covered our asses was no big deal after our year in the woods. We'd also braided our hair and tied two carved bone ornaments onto the ends. We had some goods to sell that Willow had hooked us up with, and most importantly I was wearing my cuffs. No one should be able to smell what I was, other than a wolf. The face paint and deep hood over my head should also hide my identity if I was on some wanted list.

We guided the horses up a steep hill through the last stretch of Wild Lands and I was pleased to see the small rock fence at the top indicating a territory change.

Troll Village, here we come.

"Owww wooaaaw!" an unfamiliar voice shouted a battle cry from the trees.

"Ithaki!" Sage barely got the warning out when an arrow whizzed past my head and sank into the ground, right in front of my horse. My mare reared upward as I tightened my thighs around her to hold on and gripped the reins for dear life.

Dammit! Those bastards.

Pulling a throwing knife from my thigh holster, I spun my horse around and eyed a streak of red cloth in the treetop.

"Hiya!" I spurred my horse lightly and she took off running in the direction of the Ithaki hiding in the tree. I threw my knife, and there was a yelp. A woman dressed in red rags fell backward out of the tree, clutching her chest, and hit the ground with a thud, dying instantly.

I'd killed many squirrels that way in the Dark Woods.

I relaxed a little, releasing the breath I'd been holding.

"Look out!" Sage screamed just as what felt like a boot thudded into my back and I went flying off my horse. I spun awkwardly in mid-air, falling backward just in time to see the vampire-Ithaki sailing through the air after me. He was covered in dirt camouflage, but I could smell him, that metallic vampire smell mixed with hot wires for fey magic. The air whooshed out of me as I hit the ground hard, and for a second I couldn't catch my breath. It felt like my lung collapsed, but I'd had the wind knocked out of me enough times to know that wasn't the case.

Dammit. We didn't need this, not so early in our journey. From the grunts and noises of struggle just beyond, it sounded like Sage was in her own battle. I had about two seconds to decide whether I should take off my cuffs and blast this bastard into powder but expose my scent, or keep covered and kick his butt in my human form.

I decided that he still might not know who I was and just attacked because we were wolves and he was a jerk.

'Stay covered,' my wolf agreed.

Finally, I was able to suck in a lungful of air before the bastard reached me. With a grunt, the Ithaki and I crashed together. He landed on top of me, but I was able to get my legs up in time so that he crashed into the bottom of my boots. Kicking out with all my might, I launched him off of me as he screeched, arcing through the air before he hit the ground with a thud. Knowing

I had only seconds to act or he'd be on me again with his vampire speed, I popped up onto my feet and threw myself forward. Pulling a stake from behind my back, the one I always now kept in my waist belt, I grappled with him as he reached for me.

Grabbing my right stake arm, he grunted, trying to keep me from stabbing the crap out of him. His fingers pressed so hard into my wrist that I whimpered, afraid it would snap. He was inhumanly strong, and I was very much human level strength right now, which was annoying.

'*Plan B. Take off the cuffs,*' my wolf said.

'*You read my mind,*' I growled, trying to reach for my cuff with my free arm just as the vamp-fey froze, a guttural breathy grunt leaving his lips as blood dripped from his mouth. I looked down just in time to see the front tip of a stake poking through his chest. Glancing back up, my gaze met Sage's.

"Thanks." I breathed a sigh of relief as the dude went crashing to the ground. A black network of veins crawled up his neck and his skin sank in as he started to decompose.

I studied my bestie. Sage's hair had been pulled from its braid and she was covered in dirt, same as me, but otherwise unharmed.

"Welcome," she breathed, trying to catch her breath. "I would have used the gun but didn't want to accidently shoot you."

"Appreciate that." I gave a sly smile.

Sage slung an arm around me and I chuckled. Where there was trouble, I could always count on her.

"I totally had him," I added.

"Totally." She winked.

Our horses waited just a few feet away as we scanned the trees, preparing for a possible next attack. When nothing came, I nodded. "Well, let's move on I guess."

She bobbed her head in agreement but said nothing; she didn't need to. We were both thinking it. Hopefully that attack wasn't a portent for what the rest of the trip was going to be like.

As we got onto our horses, they climbed back up the hill and jumped over the small three-foot-tall cobblestone fence that signaled our leaving the Wild Lands and entering Troll Village. We immediately came up behind a few stone buildings and into a bustling marketplace.

"Showtime," I muttered to Sage, who nodded, pulling the hood lower over her bright red hair. We both made quick work of patting off the dirt and leaves and evidence of our recent scuffle as we led the horses to an open area at the back of what looked like a market.

Trolls hurried about, running from stall after stall and buying items in a rush. Sage and I shared a look. Something wasn't right here. They were fighting each other to push to the front of the lines and acting aggressively. My head snapped to my right, where I noticed two women warring over a small jar of honey.

What in the hell is going on here?

"Traders!" someone screamed, and then the crowd turned toward us. They rushed forward, pressing in on Sage and I. My horse reared upward as I yanked her reins, clenching my thighs and trying not to get bucked off.

"Back up!" I thrust a hand out to the trolls rushing us, and they obliged.

"What have you got? Any corn?" a woman asked with desperation in her gaze.

I frowned.

This wasn't the Troll Village I'd visited over a year ago. Had the war done this? Were they low on food?

I nodded. "Blue corn. Some deer skins. And seeds."

At the mention of seeds the crowd went wild. They rushed forward, grabbing at my legs, and I was about to panic when a gunshot went off right beside me.

Everyone hit the ground, covering their ears, and I looked over at Sage, who held a sleek black handgun.

"Be calm or you get nothing!" Sage cried.

Okay, we'd agreed no guns on this trip unless absolutely necessary, but I guess that was needed lest I be torn apart by these people. I felt bad that they appeared hungry and desperate, and I wanted to help but not get hurt in the process.

Scared into compliance, they lined up one by one, single file. There must have been fifty people in total and more coming out of their houses and huts to see what was going on.

I slipped off of my horse and grabbed the trader bag that Willow had packed us. Sage stayed on her horse, gun in hand, as she stared down at the scene below.

I knelt, opening the red cloth and smoothing it into the ground as I laid my items out. There were gasps, and ohhhs and ahhhs as I arranged the seeds.

"She's got seeds!" someone said from deep in the line, and my brow furrowed again. I looked up at Sage, who held her gun trained on the crowd, and she shrugged.

The first woman came up from the line clutching an old blanket. "I'll trade you for five seeds?" She sounded unsure, like she knew it was a crappy trade. To be honest, the trader items were a front. I needed information, not a blanket.

It was a well-worn blanket too, the edges torn and frayed, and why the hell did everyone look so skinny? I didn't want to act too clueless and raise the alarm that I clearly didn't know what was going on in the magical world, but I had to find out why they looked half-starved and were fighting over seeds.

I swallowed hard, lowering my voice. "How about you tell me about why everyone needs seeds so badly? Why you are all fighting over food? Then I'll give you any five seeds you like."

Her eyes glittered with excitement at the prospect of being able to hang on to the blanket *and* the seeds. She leaned forward, nodding. "The vampires burned down all our farms nearly a year ago in order to force us to fight in the war against the wolves." She licked her lips, eyeing the broccoli, corn, squash, and carrot seeds I had.

Those bloodsucking bastards! Burned down all the farms!

Marmal.

"*All* the farms? Did you know someone named Marmal? Marmal from Rose-something." My heart pounded against my chest as I struggled to remember where my friend was from. The lady shrugged.

"Yes, all the farms, but I don't know any Marmal. Can I have my seeds?"

I nodded and she kneeled down, picking five seeds out carefully and then running off like she was escaping a fire. The man who was next looked at me quizzically.

"I know of a story about a Marmal from Rose-something. Might be your same one, but it will cost you ten seeds," he whispered.

He'd been eavesdropping.

I nodded. "Deal."

He was chubby, clearly not as starved as the others, and his nostrils were so big I could see his brain as he towered over me. The tusks in his cheeks were yellowing.

"Marmal of Rosedale was one of the first farms to burn. She lived near the vampire border." His voice was scratchy like he was a smoker.

Excitement thrummed through me. Rosedale! That was it. "Yes. That's her! Did she get away safely?"

He nodded. "She lost everything. But last I heard she'd been hired over at Trip's barn in the Dark Fey lands. She'd got a knack for animal husbandry."

Oh my God. *Marmal.* She was breeding animals for that bastard Trip in order to feed herself? In the Dark Fey lands! My mind spun with the news.

"Thank you." My voice cracked and I indicated he could take the seeds.

Leaning down, he picked out his seeds and then left, a bow and arrow tied across his back.

The next person came holding some type of family heirloom, a beautiful brooch that was an oil-rubbed bronze color and inlaid with turquoise.

"Was my mother's," she said, voice shaking. "Twenty seeds?"

I couldn't take these people's things just for food.

"Just take the seeds. Keep the brooch."

Her mouth popped open in surprise and she just stood there as if she didn't trust me.

"Come on." I waved my hand to hurry her along. I needed to get moving. I was going to give away all these seeds to these people and then I was going to see Marmal and Trip. My goal was still to find the troll who'd broken out of Magic City Prison and talk to him, but I had to check on my dear friend first.

Thinking ahead, I reached down and grabbed about fifty seeds, putting them away in my pocket in case I had to barter them with Trip for Marmal's release. I didn't know if she was a slave or an employee who could quit at any time, but I wasn't leaving her there with him.

No way.

Each person came to my little seed store and I gave each one five seeds for free. I wanted them to start their own garden and hopefully get more seeds from that and rebuild their community. The trolls were known for farming, so this was a devastating blow for them no doubt.

Once my trading cloth was empty, I packed up, and as we left, the smiles and waves as they watched us depart made me feel a little better about what we'd done.

CHAPTER TWO

"HEY, SAGE?" I CALLED OVER TO HER AS WE WOVE our horses through the grassy landscape in the direction of the barn I'd saved Astra in. We were completely avoiding Marmal's land and crisscrossing through all of Troll Village to hit the fey territories by tonight.

Sage looked over at me.

"Why doesn't the troll king get in a car and leave the Magic Lands and get some seeds from Home Depot or something?" I asked.

Sage frowned in confusion. Probably the reference to Home Depot.

"A store in the human world that sells seeds and farming stuff," I amended. "In Spokane or Idaho."

She nodded then, comprehension coming over her face. "The human hunters won't allow that kind of stuff.

Can you imagine if a human saw the troll king standing in line at a store?"

True. The only passable races in the human world were werewolves, vampires, and witches. Even then it was iffy. If we wolfed out, or a vampire's fangs distended, it was game over. Delphi had been in a magically restricted area of Spokane that humans didn't come into, and all of their stuff was delivered. Only my family and a few witch families were permitted to live off campus in normal apartment housing because we'd had the cuffs on that essentially made us human.

I shivered. "I didn't know there were human hunters. I mean, I heard rumors but I didn't believe them."

Sage nodded. "They were probably watching you the entire time you lived there. Waiting for you to slip up and expose yourself, or hurt a human, and then..." She dragged her finger across her throat.

Whoa.

I guess it was good there were rules in place to keep the humans safe from magical creatures that could get out of control.

We rode on in silence for a few hours, passing into Dark Fey Territory without an issue.

I was about to ask another question when I noticed the familiar outline of a giant pole barn in the distance. I consulted my map and nodded. "This is it, right?"

Sage bobbed her head in agreement. "We really just going to waltz in there after last time?"

I winced, remembering Walsh and I killing two of Trip's prized fighter Ithaki trolls. Walsh almost died and we'd taken Astra. It was a hot mess.

"I mean, technically, it was all part of the deal."

Sage chuckled. "Trip looked like he was ready to murder us. Let's be cautious."

She was right. The last thing I needed was for someone to turn me in to the vampires. I mulled over different ideas for ways to get inside and look for Marmal when my wolf rose to the surface.

'I'll go.'

Yes!

I was so used to not needing her that much during my time in the Dark Woods that I almost forgot she was there at times.

I clued in Sage to the plan and she nodded as we pulled our horses off to the side. We were behind some thick trees which afforded us a nice view of the back of the barn.

Sage looked at me expectantly. "Want me to shift and go with your wolf too?"

I shook my head. "No offense, but your wolf can't walk through walls."

A grin pulled at her lips. "Touché."

I slipped off my cuffs quickly and without another word, my wolf leapt out of my chest and onto the ground. She solidified and then gave me a nod as I placed the cuffs back onto my wrists.

'Find Marmal,' I told her, 'Get her to come outside.'

I was talking to myself. Of course she knew the plan, she was me. Being a split shifter would never be something I would get used to. Closing my eyes, I tuned into my wolf's point of view and suddenly I was looking out of her eyes. She padded across the rocky ground until she reached a back door.

It was closed.

Sticking her nose to it, she inhaled.

Blood. Pain. Deer. Bear. Fear.

The mixture of smells wafted through a tiny crease in the door and my wolf suddenly went semi-solid. When in my wolf form, I never had to strain to do anything or think about it too much. If I wanted to walk through a wall, I just did it. I wished my human side was more like that. Human Demi questioned everything, even herself.

When she was through the wall, she stayed semitransparent and I knew that she would be invisible to others who looked at her, the same way she'd been invisible during the meeting with the vampires, when only Sawyer saw her.

Weaving through the crowd, I noticed there was a fight going on. I recognized the yelling and the sound of fists hitting bone.

"What's happening?" Sage whispered beside me, pulling my attention from my wolf.

"She's in. There's a fight going on. She's looking

for Marmal." I slipped from my saddle. I wanted to be ready to run up and greet my troll friend.

"I'll tie off the horses," Sage informed me, and I just nodded, seeing through my wolf's eyes as she scanned the room.

Big male, small male, ugly male, Trip, animals in cages...it was all the same until I noticed a girl hunched over the largest cage in the place.

Marmal.

She was doing something to the dragon! I'd completely forgotten about the dragon creature we'd seen last time until now. My wolf burst forward, weaving in and out of the melee until she was at Marmal's heels. My beautiful troll friend was covered in dirt, on her knees and scrubbing the talons of the dragon through the cage with a bristle brush and some water. One of the talons had been shorn off completely; the end of it was flat and chipped in some spots.

"I'm sorry, girl," Marmal cooed to the dragon.

Even though my wolf was invisible, the dragon suddenly jerked her head in my direction, staring me right in the eyes. The light in the barn filtered through the bars, lighting up those milky pearl scales, and my wolf froze, entranced by her deep turquoise eyes. She was the most magnificent creature I'd ever seen.

"What's—?" Marmal said and turned her head just as my wolf solidified.

Marmal jumped a little. "Who are you? How did

you get out of your cage?" She looked over her shoulder, anxiety playing across her features as she scanned the room for Trip. My wolf stepped forward and nuzzled Marmal's leg, causing Marmal to frown. Reaching out, Marmal stroked my wolf's neck. "Come on, girl, you can't be out of the cages or I get in trouble." She dropped her scrub brush and stood, just as my wolf darted across the room.

"Get back here!" Marmal whisper-screamed, taking off after my wolf.

Now was my chance. In human form, I opened my eyes and ran from where I'd been quietly standing, near the place Sage had tied the horses off. Pumping my legs, I booked it through the trees and up to the back door of the barn, knowing that's where my wolf was going to lead Marmal.

Marmal had never met my wolf, so she wouldn't recognize her. I skidded to a stop just in front of the door at the same time my wolf leapt out of it, going from spectral to solid. The door flung open then and I was met with Marmal's bewildered face, arms outstretched to grab my wolf. The moment she looked up at me, I pulled my hood back slightly, and she paled before breaking into a grin. Slipping out the door, she glanced over her shoulder and closed it to make sure she wasn't followed.

Neither of us said anything. We both just opened our arms and pulled the other into a tight hug. It was crazy how you could bond with someone so deeply in such a short amount of time. I'd known Marmal only a few days and yet I knew I could ask anything of her. I knew that in the core of her person, she was good.

"I thought you were dead," she croaked, pulling away to get a better look at me.

My eyes trailed over a reddish scar on her right arm; it was angry and puckered and big. It looked like a burn. "I'm so sorry about your farm. Had I known, I would have—"

She cut me off, grabbing me by the armpit and pulling me away into the trees. Her eyes looked cagey, like she expected someone to come out and grab us at any moment.

"You can't be here. The bounty on your head is unfathomable." She reached up and pulled the hood back up around my face.

I frowned, an *unfathomable* bounty price was not good, but I didn't like the way she was acting, like she was scared.

"Is Trip beating you? Have they hurt you?" There was a growl in my voice and my wolf went erect beside me.

Marmal looked up at me then, shaking her head as she hugged her arms against her chest. "No, but they hurt the animals and that might as well be the same thing."

Oh God.

I shook myself. "Look, we don't have a lot of time.

I'll explain on the way. Is there anything you need to grab before we go?"

I started to back up and lead her to where Sage and our horses were. Marmal frowned, the tiny white tusks in her cheeks bent inward, making a divot into her skin.

"What?" She sounded bewildered but slightly hopeful.

"Mar, I'm not leaving you here! Sawyer is in Magic City Prison. Come with us to get him out and then you can come live in Paladin Village forever. I'm the alpha."

A slow grin pulled at her lips. "Alpha? I knew there was something special about you. Is that...your wolf? I swear I recognized the scent. You smell the same but..."

I nodded, and my wolf went spectral before leaping into my chest. Marmal staggered backward, eyes wide.

"Split shifter. Come on," I pleaded. "I'll explain on the way. There is a troll who broke out of Magic City Prison like ten years ago. Help us find him and then we can all go home together."

Marmal looked back at the barn, her brow creasing. "I...want to...but I can't leave them. I can't leave *her*."

My stomach dropped. "Who? Do you have a child? A mate?"

Marmal shook her head. "The animals, my dragon."

The moment she mentioned the dragon, my mouth dropped open. "*Your* dragon?"

Marmal's cheeks pinked. "Well, no but...I've named her and...she speaks to me."

Holy shifter! The dragon could speak to her? Maybe that was troll magic, I didn't know. But that was how I felt about Astra the moment I'd seen her, and I knew I couldn't ask Marmal to abandon the animals she had clearly grown to love over the past year. "Okay..." My mind raced trying to come up with a plan. I could tell Marmal's did the same, because she looked deep in thought.

"The troll you spoke about, who broke out of Magic City Prison...?" Marmal said.

I nodded.

"I think he came in a few months ago to see Trip, got drunk and told the guys the story. I thought he was lying to look cool," she said, and hope burst open inside of my chest.

I could barely contain my excitement. "Where does he live?"

Marmal put her hands out. "He's not pure troll. He's Ithaki, half troll and half fey."

And the hope bubble popped like a balloon. I wasn't exactly on the Ithaki's nice list right now. If I had to trek back into the Wild Lands and look for this dude, I was going to be pissed, especially after our attack.

"But he lives here. Doesn't like the Ithaki and is a loner type," she added.

And the hope was alive again. She should have started with that!

"Where?" I stepped closer, hoping she could see the desperation in my eyes.

She took in a deep breath. "I can draw you a map of the general area. I know he's in a place called South Hill, but not which cottage is his. It's a day's journey there and back."

I nodded. It was almost nightfall. We could leave first thing in the morning to go see him! "And in that time you'll find a way for us to break the animals out so you can come save Sawyer with me?" I really wanted us to be on the same page. I wasn't leaving here without her.

She grinned, nodding. "The day after tomorrow is Pearl's harvesting day. They let her out of the cage to get scales and nail clippings and…blood. I'll…I'll figure out a way to get her free then."

My heart pinched at the mention of a *harvest* day. Those bastards. I loved the name Pearl; it was perfect for her.

"My friend Sage came with me. We can help you get Pearl and all of the others out," I promised, then gestured to my redheaded bestie, who waved through the trees.

Marmal waved back; tears lined her eyes as she pulled me in for another hug. "I can't believe you came for me."

I would have come a lot sooner had I known the bad situation she was in. "Always," I promised.

When she pulled away, she pointed to my face. "Stop in a village and ask for a bridal veil before you see Seam—that's the Ithaki. I only know his first name. But

29

if he knows who you are, he'll probably just turn you in for the bounty. Troll brides wear a full face veil in public for an entire month before the wedding, only taking it off on their wedding night."

I nodded. "I will."

"He'll want a *big* payment. Gold or precious stones," she told me. "I heard him telling the guys he used to be a jeweler and was asking around for work. He's known for finding precious stones and that sort of thing."

Panic seized me at that. I didn't have gold or precious stones. I had some *seeds*. I'd been gone for so long, and with the wolves being in the bunker...I wasn't sure we had any money left. My husband was a billionaire, but I had no access to those accounts...but then my fingers went to the chain around my neck. My engagement ring. I'd put it on a necklace right before our journey. It would kill me to give this away, but if it helped Sawyer, it was worth it.

Marmal came down to where we had the horses tied and met Sage, quickly drawing a map to South Hill. There were some shops on the way where I could get a bridal veil. I thanked her and promised to be back by tomorrow night. We could sleep in the woods and then plan her escape the very next day.

Sage and I decided to push through the rest of today and get to Seam's village. We could stay at an inn or camp out in the woods. That way we wouldn't be rushed with him tomorrow, and could be back here tomorrow by nightfall.

Then it would be another day to get Marmal and her animals out...

I was cutting it pretty close given that Magic City Prison had given Sawyer seven days to live. But I didn't need to be early, I just need to get there in time.

CHAPTER THREE

THE HALF-DAY'S TREK TO SOUTH HILL PUT US THERE way past nightfall. Sage and I got the bridal veil I'd needed by trading seeds right on the troll border, and then we found an inn for the night. We tied up the horses and then brought our dinner up to the room we'd rented, before scarfing it down.

The innkeeper took one look at my full face veil and asked if I was traveling to see my new husband, and I'd just nodded, which seemed to satisfy him. We were on the border of troll and fey lands, and I'd seen a mix of both races. He took one look at Sage, inhaled, and then asked where I'd found her.

"Housemaid," I'd said, and again that seemed to satisfy him.

That night Sage and I lay snuggled in bed together and I allowed myself to think about Creek. I'd purposely not thought about my son this entire time because I'd wanted to stay focused. I wanted to be strong for Sawyer, but...

A tear slipped free and I wiped it away with the back of my hand.

Sage frowned, lying on her side, facing me. "You miss Sawyer?"

I nodded. "Also Creek."

Agony flitted across her face. "Me too. I miss the little squeaky sounds he makes when he sleeps."

I grinned, feeling better after talking about it to someone. "I love the way he smells."

Sage nodded. "Except when he poops."

We both laughed until tears leaked from our eyes. Finally, I just stared up at the ceiling until I drifted off to sleep.

———·——

'Demi!' Sawyer's voice in my head woke me from a deep sleep. My mind was foggy and my limbs were heavy with exhaustion. I looked around the room half expecting to see him before I remembered our current situation.

'I'm here,' I told him, shaking the last bits of fogginess from my brain.

'I miss you.' His voice was raw, yearning. I hadn't expected that. He seemed less rushed this time and I relaxed, lying back into the pillow.

'*I miss you. So damn much.*' My throat tightened.

'*They have a shield which keeps us from talking, but my warlock friend is able to take it down sometimes so he can contact his coven.*'

So we didn't know how long we had. I nodded, even though he couldn't see me. '*Sawyer...I...a year. I'm so sorry.*'

I'd told him three days and I was gone a year. That realization killed me.

'*You being gone this whole time has been a blessing. It's the only thing that kept me sane. It gave me hope you were still alive and the vampires hadn't gotten to you. Tell me something about your time in the woods, about Creek, I want to know everything.*'

I guess that was a good point about being safe from the vampires. '*I...can't believe I had our baby in the woods and Sage delivered him in a cabin with no electricity.*'

I could almost feel Sawyer smiling. '*You're amazing. Was the birth okay, or traumatic?*'

I considered that question. What birth wasn't traumatic to some degree? I had nothing to compare it to, but from what I knew it was pretty textbook. '*Normal. I had to carry around his placenta in a bowl because we were too scared to cut it.*'

He laughed, a deep throaty laugh that reverberated in my head and made me miss him so much it physically hurt. It felt like a weight sat on my chest and pinched my heart. '*I gotta get you a push present when I get out.*'

I giggled and looked at Sage to make sure she was still sleeping. *'How do you know what a push present is?'*

'They let us watch human movies in here,' Sawyer said.

I played with the ring at the chain on my throat. *'Tell me about your past year. Walsh is there?'*

'Yeah, the idiot followed me in here. I don't deserve him.'

I nodded, staring at a sleeping Sage, and wondered what I did to deserve her.

'Is it…rough in there?' I asked. I mean regular prison was rough, I couldn't imagine prison with supernaturals who could kick your butt with magic.

He was quiet, like he wasn't sure he wanted to say anything.

'Sawyer. Tell me.' I couldn't feel much through our bond. Either he was tightening it up or some magic wasn't letting things through.

'I'm surviving,' he finally said. *'They make us all wear the cuffs you grew up with. The ones that cause pain if you try to shift.'* There was shame in his voice and I knew he felt guilty at knowing I wore those nearly every day of my life for over twenty years.

'I'm sorry,' I told him honestly. Keeping your wolf at bay for a year sucked, especially for an alpha. *'Are there many fights?'*

I suddenly felt protective of my man and I wanted to know what he'd been dealing with.

'*Every day,*' he finally answered. '*But I've created my own little pack in here. Don't worry about me. Focus on keeping yourself safe. Keeping our baby safe.*'

It sounded like Sawyer had created some little pack gang to survive prison. My, my, how things had changed. I frowned at his telling me to just focus on keeping myself and Creek safe. '*I'm focused on getting you out of there. I'm in Dark Fey Territory right now, meeting a guy named Seam who broke out of Magic City Prison ten years ago.*'

Something spiked through our bond. Fear. '*You're in Dark Fey lands? Where's Creek? The packs?*'

I wanted to roll my eyes, but then remembered what it felt like to be in the woods for a year cut off from all information. Sawyer knew nothing about what had been going on. '*Creek is with my mom and they are all in Paladin Village with both of our packs. Everyone is safe because I'm an alpha and I'm good at my job.*' I all but growled at my man.

'*Damn, you're sexy when you're mad,*' Sawyer said, and I could almost see him grinning, which lightened my mood. '*You're right, you know what you're doing. I just hate not being there.*'

I could imagine, especially for an alpha. '*I got everything covered. Including getting you out of prison,*' I told him.

'*Seam, you said? That guy's a legend here.*'

'*Yep. Him.*' I brightened knowing he recognized the guy.

'*Demi, that is a really good plan...but that dude broke out before they went all high-tech with the place. There is literally no way you can get me out of here, my love. Not without alerting half the magical community.*' He was quiet. '*Demi, I've seen Queen Drake here. I've heard them talk about me, asking if they thought I was talking to anyone or passing notes to Walsh about you. They are waiting for you.*'

Anger flared up inside of me. '*Screw Queen Drake, I just stabbed that hag in the shoulder a few nights ago. Sawyer, I need you to believe in me. I need you to be ready to blow that joint, because I'm coming whether you like it or not.*'

He was silent for too long, so long I thought I'd lost him. Maybe our connection was lost and his warlock friend couldn't bring down the signal jammer anymore or whatever. Just when I was ready to fall back asleep, he spoke again.

'*You're sexy when you're plotting prison breaks. I'll be ready. I love you.*'

'*I love you too,*' I said, grinning, and then suddenly the connection was broken. I felt Sawyer leave me, taking his familiar presence with him.

I lay back on the bed, staring up at the peeling plaster ceiling, and sighed.

Love made you lose your mind, made you do wild things, but if I could rewind to that day at Delphi where Sawyer and I first met, I wouldn't take it back. I wouldn't take any of this back. I loved the person that loving Sawyer had made me. I was a strong woman, an alpha, a mother. None of that I would have known if he hadn't found me and broken me out of my Delphi prison, out of my cuffs. Now it was time for me to return the favor.

———·—·—

I tossed and turned after talking to Sawyer until finally morning light came. After washing up and having breakfast, I slipped into my troll bridal veil and we set out for Seam's house. We asked a grumpy female dark fey from South Hill where Seam the Ithaki lived and she just pointed to a tiny blue cabin on the top of the hill and grunted.

The horses made slow work of going up the hill, so much so I was tempted to just tie them up at the bottom and walk up, but I wasn't sure if they would be stolen. When we finally reached a set of rusted steel gates, I stared at the sign tied to the gate. The paint was peeling, but I could make out the words clearly. *Get out*, it read.

I looked at Sage.

"I can't see your face right now, but I'm guessing you don't like the sign." Sage tried to peer through the tiny dots poked in the cream cotton veil and see my expression.

"Correct. Don't like it one bit. We have no idea what

kind of dude this might be. Should I have my wolf come out and walk in with us?"

She tapped her chin. "That's threatening. We need to seem meek. If we get into trouble you can yank your cuffs off and we'll fight our way out."

I nodded. That was a decent plan. It would lead the vampires to us, but decent.

"Here goes nothing, then." I stepped up to the gate and reached out to grasp the handle. The second my fingers touched the cool metal, a shock ripped through my arm and I yanked it back with a yelp.

"Bastard!" I screamed.

It was electrified!

"What do you want?" a deep, ominous voice called out from somewhere in the bushes.

Damn.

I spun, looking at the bush, and then relaxed a little when I saw a speaker. It was very untroll-like to have what Marmal referred to as "demon technology," but I was guessing this Ithaki was more fey-like. Dark fey, I had to remind myself. The bad ones.

I stepped closer to the bush. "I want to give you this fat shiny diamond in exchange for information," I called back, pulling the ring from my hand and holding it up to the house. I'd moved it from my necklace to my wedding finger this morning. I saw a curtain move and then the gate opened with a loud creak.

Gotcha.

Greed was good. I could work with that.

We left the horses tied to the bottom gatepost and headed up the driveway on foot. The house was in major disrepair, which was a good sign that he needed money. This boded well for him taking my ring in exchange for information. The blue siding was warped and the roof was metal but rusted. The place was definitely not well taken care of, that was for sure.

By the time we reached the front door, it stood open and a tall man lurked in the entryway. His hair was white and hung halfway down his back; he had small cheek tusks and pointy fey ears. He didn't look like a dark fey. In fact, he looked very much like he was half-light fey. His white hair and crisp blue eyes were telltale signs…but then why live here? Among the evil?

He was slender and tall, definitely more fey than troll in stature. One long arm hung to his side and another shorter arm, missing the hand, he held to his chest.

"Jewel?" He held out his good hand.

"Information first." I tucked the ring into my palm.

He rolled his eyes. "Obviously, but I need to see the jewel to make sure it's real."

I pulled the ring off my finger, saying a silent goodbye, and held it out to him. He reached out and extended a bony finger toward me. The nails were sharpened to points and painted black. Maybe a disguise so he would fit in with the other fey in town.

I was suddenly wondering what he did to land himself in Magic City Prison. Snaking the ring from my hand, he held it up to the light, grinning.

Pointed teeth.

Okay...he was part dark fey...good thing I was under this veil because I couldn't control my reactions right now.

"Five carats?" He pulled out a magnifying glass.

I stepped forward. "Uh, I guess so. It's worth at least a hundred grand," I guessed.

Sage sidled next to me. "Half a million. It's colorless, flawless, and round cut by a master jeweler in Paris."

I could see the physical greed come over Seam at Sage's words. His eyes practically glittered as he rolled the gem in his hand.

Half a million! Whoa. I looked at my bestie with surprise.

"I helped him pick it out." She winked at me.

The man handed me the ring and I shoved it back on my finger. "What knowledge do you require for such an impressive payment?"

I took in a deep breath. "I need to know how to break someone out of Magic City Prison."

The Ithaki considered me for a long moment, just staring at me through the holes in my veil. "Fine. It's your funeral."

"I'll need you to give me your word, sir. You will give me all of the information you have on Magic City

41

Prison, including maps of the buildings, in exchange for this ring." I held up my hand.

He was fey, and I knew with fey that words were important.

He smirked, crossing his arms. "I promise to give you all of the information I have on Magic City Prison, including maps of the buildings in exchange for *that* ring." He pointed to my hand and I relaxed a little. "Oh, and you can take off the veil. I know who you are and that you've come to try and break out Sawyer Hudson." Then he turned on his heel and walked into the house.

Sage went rigid beside me and I froze, looking at her in shock.

Damn.

How did he know?

"Come along!" he shouted, and we scrambled inside after him.

Well, no sense wearing this sweaty thing if he knew who I was already.

I ripped off the veil and gasped for air as a cool breeze touched my skin. Sage stared at me and I shrugged. We still had our plan that if things got shady I could rip off my cuffs and fight him.

The fey walked deeper into the foyer, to a set of glass doors that led to a garden, and turned to face us. The second he laid eyes on my veil-less face, the color drained from his complexion and his gaze flicked to a picture on the entry table.

I followed his gaze and saw a photo with a younger Seam. A little girl was perched on his shoulder. She had the same white-blond hair as him.

"I don't have all day," he snapped, and opened the doors, stepping out into the garden.

I tore my gaze from the photo, wondering where the little girl was now. She was clearly his daughter, they looked so much alike. Sage and I ran through the dingy foyer with peeling paint walls and warped wood floors before following him into the courtyard outside. There was a large table set up with a steaming hot teacup and a plate of food. We'd interrupted his breakfast.

"How did you know?" I asked him, taking in the courtyard and looking for exits in case he attacked. There was a white picket fence only three feet high that I could easily climb over. There were also dozens of beautiful rose bushes that dotted the edge of the red brick patio. The outside garden had clearly been maintained, whereas the inside had been left to rot.

Seam sat down, sipping his tea and then finishing off a cookie. "You travel with a werewolf..." He gestured to Sage: "You have a half-a-million-dollar ring, and you want to break someone out of Magic City Prison the day after they announce all over the news that Sawyer Hudson is sentenced to death."

Dammit. He was right—it was so obvious.

"Why not call the vampires, get the bounty?" Sage asked, her hand twitching at her hip where her sword was.

He rolled his eyes, taking a bite of a cucumber sandwich. "Did you see what they did to my homeland?" He gestured out beyond his yard, down at the base of the backside of the hill. He lived right on the fey border, but you could see Troll Village from here, and the farmlands. Once so beautiful with their golds and greens, everything was now black as far as the eye could see. "They burned it all. I'm not keen on giving them anything they want anytime soon. Besides, that ring will easily fix this place up and I can retire early. I don't need much here."

Okay…it was a decent answer, but I wasn't going to trust it. He could turn on me at any time and I was going to treat him as such.

"How did you escape?" I asked. "Tell me everything."

He eyed the two chairs on the other side of the table. "Sit, this will take a while."

CHAPTER FOUR

TWO HOURS LATER, WE'D HEARD THE ENTIRE STORY. Magic City Prison was built up eighty stories into the sky. It was the tallest building in Magic City, which was in downtown Light Fey Territory, and the prisoners were all kept on the upper fifty floors. The lower thirty floors were for administration, storage, and other things. It was almost as tall as the freaking Eiffel Tower! But the worst news I heard was that it was on a tiny sandbank island in the middle of a giant roaring river. You had to swim or take a boat to get to the building.

"So even the lowest level is two hundred feet in the sky," I observed as he described the layout.

He nodded. "Can't jump out that window without certain death."

I squirmed as I stared at the nub on the end of his

arm. He'd recounted his story of cutting off his own hand to release the cuff's magic. "So they only had one cuff before?" I asked for the fifth time.

He bobbed his head. "And now they do both arms *and* legs."

Damn. Maybe Sawyer was right and this was hopeless. Seam had told us that there was a magical grid built into the building, and even if you did make it out, you couldn't leave the property with the cuffs still on or you'd die instantly. So I'd need to get Sawyer's and Walsh's cuffs off and then break them out somehow.

I decided to leave that for later and focus on any other information I could use. "So after you...?" I looked at his handless arm.

He grinned. "I lured the guard in and knocked him out."

I nodded, replaying the story he'd just told us. "And you then dragged his body over to the cell and used his handprint to unlock the door because the doors lock behind them..."

He nodded. "Once I was in the hallway, I climbed into the air conditioning shaft, which I'd noticed was loose after a routine maintenance."

Sage bobbed her head. "Because normally they are bolted shut."

We'd been over this ten times, trying to find something we could use for Sawyer.

"Precisely. And then I climbed thirty floors down

through the narrow venting until I hit the underground parking lot."

"From there you stole a boat. All of this is likely not going to help us since after you left, they have tightened security."

Frick.

He looked at me seriously, stroking his chin with his good hand. "Is it true that you're a cursed one? Demon? Soul jumper?"

I swallowed hard. Soul jumper? That was new. "No. I don't know what that is," I lied immediately.

His eyes glittered as if he didn't believe me. "Because if the rumors are true, you could just have your wolf soul jump into your little friend here..." He pointed to Sage. "...and then she could get you inside the building. Two-for-one special."

I frowned. What was he talking about?

Sage leaned forward. "What do you mean?"

The Ithaki rolled his eyes. "Her wolf, if the rumor is true, it jumped out of her body before with cuffs on, so surely it can do it again. She can't get arrested because the Magic City warden will just turn her over to Queen Drake, but you..." He appraised Sage. "You they would gladly take in."

A light dawned on me. "Trojan horse."

He slammed his good hand down on the table and we both jumped. "Exactly!"

Sage could sneak my wolf into the building and then

I could pull her out and...somehow free them all. But I could never ask Sage to do that, risk her life like that.

"Well, if the rumors were true, which they're not, that would be a good idea," Sage said, giving me the wide "let's talk later" eyes.

I looked at Seam, wondering why the hell he was giving us these good ideas when he so clearly could turn me in or worse, try to "steal my essence" like everyone else I'd met along the way.

"What's your deal? Why are you helping me?" I crossed my arms over my chest, eyeing him with suspicion. We'd been here over two hours and he'd done nothing but answer all of my questions. He'd pulled out maps with hand-drawn hallways and riverways. He'd gone above and beyond. But if he was going to alert someone and turn me in, he'd have done it by now. Two hours was more than enough time for the vampires to come knocking.

His face turned dark, eyes narrowing. "The diamond obviously." But his gaze ran over my long white hair and his face softened. There was something else there.

The girl, from the photo. Her hair was like mine, long and thick and silvery blond.

"Nothing else?" I pressed.

He sighed, looking over at the wall of pink roses. He was quiet for a long time, chest rising and falling with each breath. I don't think he had many visitors and he might actually be enjoying our company. He hadn't asked us to leave and had even offered us tea. We both declined on account of not trusting him, but now I wondered if he was just misunderstood.

"I had a daughter. You remind me of her," was all he said, and my heart pinched. It was as I thought.

I noticed the past tense. He *had* a daughter.

"I'm sorry," I told him earnestly.

"What happened?" Sage asked.

I kicked her under the table and she winced.

He looked at Sage, seemingly considering her question and if he wanted to answer it.

"I'm never going to see you again after this so…" He shrugged. "Why not?"

Then he leaned in, letting the sun shine on his face, and peeling back his lips he showcased his razor sharp teeth.

We both reeled back a little, unsure what he was doing and he chuckled. "Are you not confused with my lineage? I have the teeth of a dark fey, hair and eyes of a light fey, and the tusks of a troll."

Ohhh, as soon as he said it, it clicked. He was…a total mix of many races.

"Your mother or father was both?" I asked.

He nodded. "Mother was half light and half dark fey. Father was troll. I have the lineage of all three. Never quite belonged but I never bothered anyone, so they didn't seem to mind. Then I met my wife…"

His voice broke as he looked again at the wall of flowers.

The roses. The garden so lovingly cared for...it was his wife's?

"She was a vampire-fey Ithaki," he stated and my mouth popped open. The fey were the only ones who could breed with the other races. They had some kind of gene that could morph either way and create life where none could be created naturally.

"So your daughter..." Sage put it all together in her mind before I did.

He inclined his head. "She was a true chimera. Dark fey, light fey, vampire, and troll. She had untold power when I started to train her..."

His voice trailed off and he looked at me. I knew then what had happened without him even having to say it. Power was something that the vampires, specifically Queen Drake, couldn't allow.

I growled. "They took her?"

He nodded. "The vampires took her, experimented on her, killed her."

The veins in his neck popped and the ring of the teacup snapped as he held it too tightly, then dropped to the floor and shattered, spilling its contents. "Sorry, I haven't spoken about this in a long time."

The fear I'd once held of him, the mistrust, it vanished in that moment. This was just a broken old man. I dropped by his feet and started to pick up the teacup shards. "It's fine," I told him. "So is that...why you went to prison? You retaliated?"

He nodded. "Sort of. Justice system was taking too long for my wife's liking."

That sounded familiar.

"When my wife and I got news from the local authorities that they'd found our sweet sixteen-year-old daughter's body on vampire land in a shallow ditch with a bunch of holes in her arms and completely drained of blood..." The knuckles in his one hand popped as he made a fist. "We pressed charges, but they said it could take up to a year to find the killer. Magic City Police don't care about Ithaki. Some lowly vampire, they said it probably was. I knew that wasn't true. The queen had been poking around here once she got word of my daughter and her power. Even offered to pay us for her."

Sage gasped. "Pay you!"

He nodded. "Under the guise that it was some fancy private education, but I could smell the hunger on her when she looked at my sweet girl." His eyes glistened with moisture in the sunlight and my heart ached for him. If it were possible to hate this bitter queen any more, I did. I wanted her wiped from this earth.

"So, your wife is...gone?" Sage asked.

We were too far into the story to stop now. I needed to know everything. I set the broken teacup pieces on the table and returned to my seat as he nodded his thanks to me.

"Varilla was a fearsome warrior. When she heard about our daughter, she stopped sleeping. One night,

I found her gone, bed empty and a note saying she wouldn't rest until the queen was dead."

Oh crap.

Sage reached out and grasped my hand and squeezed.

"I ran all night, used every magical power I had to get into the Vampire City walls and to where the queen's castle was, but I was too late. My wife was dead, the queen wasn't even in town, but my wife had killed a dozen of her guards before they took her down. They arrested me for trespassing and attempted murder of a monarch."

Holy crap.

His wife and daughter all gone within a week…

"I'm so sorry," I told him, my voice breaking.

He leaned inward. "I begged them to kill me, but the queen ordered that I live my life without the two women I love as my punishment."

Evil woman.

"So why even break out? I mean…you didn't really have anyone to come home to?" Sage said, and then winced at her wording. "I mean, that's not what I meant. I—"

He waved her off with his good hand. "No, you're right. I came back for those." He pointed to the wall of perfectly manicured flowers. "My wife loved few things as much as she loved me and our daughter, and those roses are one of them. She spent hours out here. I couldn't bear the thought of them dying too. Something she put so much of her life into."

A tear slipped from my eye and trailed down my cheek before I could blink it back. It was the saddest thing I'd ever heard, and yet...kind of beautiful. He'd let the house go, but he'd kept up the flowers.

"They're beautiful flowers," I told him. "And if it makes you feel any better, I plan on killing Queen Drake very, very soon."

I was dead serious and he appraised me with one raised eyebrow.

"So it's true. What her son did? That whole family is evil. Tainted," he hissed. "It would make me feel a whole hell of a lot better if you'd mail me her ashes once she was dead. That way I could mix them with clay and make a urinal out of them, piss on it every day."

I burst into laughter; Sage did the same beside me. He grinned. And that was that. We all had something in common. That damn queen was going to die if it was the last thing I did.

He waved me off. "Well, you all better get going. I'll get the rest of the maps and then you can be on your way."

I nodded. He was a nice man. I'd totally underestimated him.

He returned a few minutes later with a stack of maps in his arms. "These are copies. You can have them."

I thanked him before slipping the ring off my finger and handing him the one physical memory of my marriage to Sawyer that I had left. "Thanks for your help," I told him.

He stared at the ring, pausing. "I really do need this. Otherwise, I'd—"

I waved him off, looking at his broken-down house and sad life. "Don't worry. Sawyer can get me another." I smiled.

It was a half-truth. Yes, Sawyer could get me another ring. It wouldn't be the same one, with all the beautiful memories, but it didn't matter. A deal was a deal, and I wanted Seam to have a good life after all that he'd been through.

He closed his hand around it and nodded. "Well, all right then. Be safe and good luck."

"Keep your eye on the mailbox." I winked, which caused him to grin.

He walked us out through the house, but when we stood in the doorway about to go, his arm snaked out and he pulled me near him. "There will come a time in this daring escape when you have to ask yourself how badly you want to get him out." Then his gaze fell to the long scar at the end of his sawed-off hand. "Sacrifices may have to be made."

I swallowed hard and nodded. Message received. I just hoped it wouldn't come to that.

When Sage and I reached the horses at the bottom of the hill, I looked up at the crumbling old house.

"That was not how I expected it to go," I told her.

She nodded. "He was…kinda sweet."

He was just a grieving dad and husband trying to get back to his wife's dying roses in time.

"Demi, I know you're going to try to protect me and say no, but if you think it's possible for your wolf to…" She shivered a little. "…join my body, then I want to try that. I want to save my cousin."

I nodded. I'd already done a check-in with my wolf and she thought it was possible. "I've got an idea…" I told her.

Sage swung one leg over her horse and grinned at me. "I'm all ears."

I blew air out through my teeth. "So, for starters, we're going back to Trip's animal barn and stealing that dragon. You game?"

She grinned. "Ride or die."

I just hoped Marmal would be okay with my using Pearl in a prison escape.

———— • · • ————

It took us the rest of the day to get back across the fey lands and to Trip's barn. Marmal met us in the meetup spot we'd previously discussed, and an idea hatched in the flickering lamplight of the tent we all shared deep in the woods.

"So, after we get Sage arrested and she gets inside the prison," I told them, "I'll let my wolf out of her and she'll find Sawyer."

Seam had confirmed what Sawyer had told me, which is that my wolf wouldn't be able to just walk through the outside walls and into the prison, because of the protection magic there, but she could walk through the interior walls he thought.

"Once I find Sawyer and Walsh, my wolf breaks them out by attacking a guard and using his key to unlock their cuffs," I said.

Without those cuffs off, there was no use in trying to get them out of there. The magical grid would kill them instantly, and I wasn't messing with that.

Marmal and Sage nodded, wide-eyed. "Then we rendezvous with Sage, break out the window and jump onto Pearl's back that Marmal will be flying."

I looked at my troll friend to see what she thought of the idea and her mouth hung open, slack jawed. I hadn't exactly asked her about this yet…

"Say what now?" Marmal blinked rapidly at me.

Okay, I should have probably eased her into the plan better, but I was really excited. "The vampires will be waiting for us. The second the alarm sounds that we are breaking people out of their cells, the whole place will go into lockdown," I told her.

"So you jump out of a window eighty floors up?" Marmal looked at me like I'd lost my mind. "I'm not even sure Pearl can fly, and if she can, I'm not sure she can fly that high!"

I let out the breath I'd been holding. "Look, I've

run through this in my head a hundred different ways and this is the only one I can think of that gives us a chance. They'll use magic to bring down a helicopter, but a damn dragon! That will confuse their witches and give us a chance."

Marmal chewed her lip. "Dragons are actually impervious to magic, you can't spell them."

Hope blossomed in my chest, that was the best news I'd heard in a long time. "Do you think you can get her to fly once we get her out?"

Marmal blew air through her teeth. "She's been captive for *years*. They use her strictly for DNA donation. Trip does dark magic, binding the animals to fey so that they can speak into the animals' minds and control them. That's what Trip's little breeding barn is all about. I...I don't know if she can fly, they don't let her outside the barn." There was anger in her voice and she had good reason for it. Those bastards had been treating that dragon like a lab rat, treating all of those animals like that. How dare they!

"Well, we can get a cart to hook up to Sage and my horses and carry her on that until she heals, or until you can practice with her?" It would also help to hide her until the moment we needed her. A fifteen-foot-long dragon wasn't easy to conceal.

Marmal nodded. "Okay, it's worth a try, but no promises."

I bopped my hands excitedly on my legs, eager for

this plan and what tomorrow would bring. A *try* was all I needed.

"But we have to break her out first," Marmal added.

I inclined my head. "You leave that to me and my wolf."

I didn't know a lot about troll magic, they were so secretive about it, but I knew they could manipulate metals and were master blacksmiths. "Marmal, can you...open the locks of the cages without touching them?" *Like with your magic,* I wanted to say but didn't.

She suddenly became very shy, cheeks reddening as she looked down at her hands. It was super taboo in their culture to talk about their magic. I had no idea why. Something about the chance that they would lose it or something if I remembered my troll history and culture correctly.

"Because if you could..." I added, "we could free *all* of the animals, not just Pearl, and it would create the distraction we'd need to get Pearl out."

She swallowed hard and then nodded once. I was going to take that as a yes.

Those bastards were going to pay for what they were doing to these defenseless animals. I'd make sure of it.

CHAPTER FIVE

THE NEXT MORNING I AWOKE WITH A DESPERATE fever to get to Sawyer. I hadn't heard from him no matter how many times I'd reached out, and because we were in the middle of Dark Fey Territory, we had no access to a radio or anything for me to know what was going on in Light Fey City, where the jail was. Marmal had crept out of the tent early this morning for her daily shift at Trip's barn. Sage and I would go in a few minutes and steal a cart and buggy to tie our horses up to. Then we'd start a fire at the back door to create the distraction she'd need to work her untold magic and open those cages. It was a solid plan, assuming nothing went wrong.

'How's the pack?' I did a quick check-in with Rab. He'd been keeping me abreast with little comments here and there through our connection, but it didn't work in

Troll Village, so I could only talk to him here in the fey lands.

'*Good. Had an issue with the water tank. It's cracked, but we got it fixed and morale is high. Everyone loves being outdoors.*'

That was a huge relief. I wasn't sure what I would do if he told me there was a big problem and I had to come home.

'*How's my mom doing with Creek?*' I tried not to think about my baby, but it was hard, I missed him so damn much it hurt. I felt emotional whenever I thought about him too much, so I just tried to push him from my mind.

'*Great, Willow is helping her, and Creek and Daisy have become best friends.*'

I smiled, a tear slipping down my cheek at that.

'*Hunting going okay?*' I switched gears. Twenty thousand people was a lot to feed. We'd brought what dwindling provisions they had from the bunker, but it wouldn't last long. My magic seemed to have healed the land, but I wasn't sure how that translated into actual food to feed that many people.

'*We are already smoking elk meat in excess,*' he replied. '*The blueberry fields are ripe with fruit.*'

Another relief.

'*Astra? Is she okay?*'

'*Alpha, everything is fine here. Astra is well and walking among the people again. Don't worry. I'll*

60

contact you if we have a problem. You just focus on bringing your mate back.'

I sighed in relief again. 'You're the best. Thank you.'

After that, I met up with Sage and helped her break down the tent. A tent was a luxury compared to what we'd gone through in the Dark Woods. Water treatment tablets, freeze dried food, all the stuff she'd packed was way more than we needed out there.

"Thinking about our time in the woods?" she asked as she shoved the tent into the saddlebag on the horse.

I nodded. "Do you miss it?"

She chuckled. "I do. Is that weird? I mean the woods were constantly trying to kill me, and before I met up with you, I was starving half the time, and scared, but then…there was a peace there, ya know? Our little cabin by the creek."

I bobbed my head. "I know."

"But let's not *ever* go back there." Sage scrunched her face and I laughed.

A pang of sadness struck through my chest at that: never see the cabin where I birthed Creek again? I guess not, huh? Why would I ever go back there?

"But we could build you and Sawyer a little cabin on the creek in Paladin Village," Sage offered, probably noticing my sadness.

I beamed. I hadn't really gotten to explore Paladin Village as much as I'd liked to. I knew there was a creek and so much farmland to explore. I was alpha of a place I hadn't really spent much time in.

"I'd like that," I told her, my bottom lip trembling as I suddenly became emotional.

"Hey." Sage gripped my shoulders. "We're going to get Sawyer back. I promise."

I nodded, wiping my cheek. Now that I'd envisioned a house on the creek with Sawyer and our son, I didn't want to give that future up.

"Now, let's go steal a horse buggy," I said, and we both burst into laughter.

Sage grinned. "So many things I never thought we would casually say."

With our mood lightened, we walked our horses over to the thick trees behind the barn and tied them up. Then we hiked up to the back door and around the side to a large storage shed that Marmal had told us held the wagons.

"Time to walk through a wall," I told Sage as we ducked behind the storage shed. I could hear two men talking at the front, so I was going to send my wolf in first.

I pulled off my cuffs for two seconds and my wolf jumped out of my body and through the wall like it was no big deal, then I slipped the cuffs back on quickly. Shifting my awareness to hers, I was suddenly looking at a giant storehouse of animal saddles, bridles, cages, and carts and wagons of varying size. This was exactly what we needed! The giant front double doors were wide open, but two men were standing there talking loudly and clearly hadn't smelled or heard my wolf.

The two men were very large. We were going to need a small distraction to lure them away, not one that would tip them off that we were about to ambush the place but enough to make them run off into the woods for a few minutes so I could get the wagon out.

I wished I could mentally talk to Sage in human form. It was annoying to have to whisper as a human and try not to be heard.

"Get ready to run with the wagon," I nearly mouthed, trying to speak as low as possible to her as she stood beside me. She nodded and I blinked back to my wolf's awareness.

She already knew the plan, since we shared the same mind.

'Be safe,' I told her.

'I'm faster than them,' she replied.

My wolf totally had an ego. Or I did, I guess. Great.

Without wasting another second, my wolf solidified and slammed into a nearby cage to make it rattle. Both men stopped talking and spun, just as she darted out of the barn between their legs.

"Oy! A wolf got loose from the barn!" one of the men said and took off running after her.

The second man stayed where he was, watching the scene unfold. My wolf pounded the ground as fast as she could, and it was clear the one dude wasn't going to be able to catch up with her.

Come on, go help your buddy, I thought.

"That damn troll woman is useless!" the second man growled, slamming the double doors of the shed shut and taking off into the woods.

"Let's go!" I whisper-screamed to Sage and pulled my attention fully to my human form. We burst around the front of the storage shed and yanked the doors back, running inside. We needed something big, big enough to carry Pearl and us and not break our horses' backs.

"That one!" Sage hissed, and we ran over to a large sturdy wooden carriage. It was tented with some type of lightweight material that would conceal us.

Perfect.

It had four giant wheels, and then two long poles to connect to the horses' saddles. I grabbed one stick and Sage grabbed the other and then we heaved it forward.

Holy Mother.

This thing was heavy, but it was our only way through Dark Fey Territory until we could steal a car in Light Fey.

Come on…

Inch by inch, we heaved it forward, stopping to move other junk out the way. We were too slow, I could hear the men's far-off voices, and knew they might just give up on catching my wolf and come back. Without a second thought, I ripped off the cuffs, shoving them into my cloak pocket, feeling my magic flaring to life under my skin. With a grunt, I yanked the wagon forward and dragged it at super speed out of the storage shed.

"Whoa!" Sage yelled and scrambled to get out of the way as I almost dragged her under it.

"Sorry," I whisper-screamed, unaware of how much strength and speed I had at the moment. I dragged the cart behind the shed and back down the hill to where our horses were grazing while Sage covered our tracks behind me. Magic pulsed through my body in electric waves and my heart pounded in my chest. I felt like the Hulk on steroids.

When I finally stopped, panting and feeling light-headed, I slipped on the cuffs quickly and looked at my friend. She was watching me with wide eyes.

"The *hell* was that?" She looked at my arms as if she expected them to grow in size.

I laughed nervously. "Magic, I guess."

Sage just shook her head. "Incredible, your powers are getting stronger."

Were they? Or was I just starting to discover them all? Since the moment I found out what I was, everyone was trying to suppress my powers or hide them. I wondered if I was able to just be free and use them, what I would be capable of. I probably should have tried in the woods, but I was too busy learning to trust my human side and getting food and looking for the cave to bother with magic.

"Okay, you hook up the horses, I'll go start the fire and then get ready to scram," I told my bestie and second-in-command.

She nodded and got to work tying our horses to the wagon. My wolf pulled at my attention and I focused on her, seeing that she'd allowed the men to catch her. She growled as they pulled her into the front doors of the barn with a rope around her neck. The big dude then handed the rope to Marmal, who was bent in front of Pearl's cage. She had a special key in her hand and was opening the lock. She'd told us last night that on Pearl's "harvesting" day she was permitted to use the key to take Pearl out and bring her to the back room. She'd worked there a year and they trusted her to do this alone now without an escort. She wasn't able to open the lock with her magic, as it had some type of protective spell over it that the others did not.

"Keep the damn animals in the cage or I'll have you fired!" the troll-fey Ithaki snapped at Marmal, handing her the rope-leash that was connected to my wolf.

She took one look at my wolf, eyes widening slightly, and nodded curtly to the man.

Good. My wolf was safe with her, and she'd gotten the key to let Pearl out. Time to light this place up.

Literally.

Scrambling up the hill to the back barn door, I pulled out the lighter and kindling from my pocket that I'd stashed there earlier this morning. Shoving the kindling into a crack in the wooden siding of the barn, I lit it, blowing softly to increase the flame. It caught and slowly flickered up the wall, causing tendrils of smoke to waft up to the sky.

Okay, now to throw some fuel on that fire.

Pulling out the small bottle of fuel Marmal had given me, I stood back and popped off the lid.

Here goes nothing.

I threw the liquid, dousing the bottom half of the flames. For a second I feared they would go out, but then the fire roared to life and engulfed the entire back wall of the barn in seconds. I stumbled backward as the heat became too intense, the crackling and popping growing louder.

Time to scram.

Running to the side of the barn, I pulled my hood up as I heard a commotion inside.

"Fire!" I heard someone yell.

I snapped my attention to my wolf, who was still inside the barn, and was immediately assaulted by the smell of smoke. Marmal was in the corner near Pearl's unlocked cage, looking at the ceiling like she was in a trance. My wolf was curled protectively around her feet, staring up at her. The scent of hot wires and burning electricity filled the air.

Magic. Troll magic.

Click, *click*, *click*, the sound of hundreds of locks opening clattered throughout the space like an orchestra.

The fire had fully engulfed the entire back wall, including Trip's office, and people now abandoned all thoughts of putting it out as they fled for the exit.

"Magic!" someone yelled, and that's when Marmal stepped over to the door of Pearl's cage and pulled it wide open.

My wolf tipped her head back and howled, long and deep, and I felt a stirring in the air, as if she'd somehow sent out a signal to the other animals that it was time to fight and be free. The animals had gotten wind of the fact that their cages had been unlocked, and now they butted the cage doors open with their snouts. Marmal's magic was so powerful, she'd unlocked every single cage. I was in complete awe of her.

A gray plume of smoke filled the barn so quickly I worried they wouldn't get out in time. Dozens of different animals leapt out into the commotion, all abandoning their cages. Foxes, bears, wolves, otters, eagles, it was wild.

"Come on!" Marmal screamed as she yanked Pearl's neck. The dragon looked afraid, like she wasn't sure if they were going to do another experiment on her. "I promise," Marmal said with a fierce look, peering into Pearl's eyes. "Never again. You're free."

With that, Pearl stood, climbing out of the giant cage and standing to her full height just outside of it.

Holy snakebite.

She was huge. Like...*definitely not going to fit in*

the wagon huge. She stood over twenty feet high, her head almost touching the barn roof, and her wings weren't even outstretched yet. Her gaze darted around the burning barn with paranoia, and then suddenly she swooped down, grabbing the back of Marmal's shirt with her teeth and lifted her into the air with a squeal. Flicking her head backward, she tossed Marmal onto her back and then took off for the open doors, running on her talons.

Holy crap.

'Get out of there,' I told my wolf. Pearl clearly had an instinct to protect Marmal, but not my wolf, whom she didn't know from any other animal there.

My wolf ran for the entrance, where I was waiting as people and animals passed me in a panic. She darted through the terrified animals like she was stuck in a maze, when suddenly a sharp pain shot up her back as someone grasped her by the skin and lifted. The second Trip pulled my wolf to his face and sniffed her, my human self tried to rush forward and help her, but there were so many people blocking the entrance in their urgency to escape.

"You look familiar," he growled to my wolf, walking quickly toward the exit as his barn burned behind him and the freed animals ran for their lives.

Switching back to my human perspective, I looked over my shoulder to try to locate Sage or Marmal, and gasped when I saw a shiny blur of white take off into the sky above me.

Pearl had gotten out, and now she *flew*, with Marmal on her back!

"Follow them!" I yelled down the embankment at Sage, who was riding as fast as she could on our horse and buggy to get up to the main road. I wasn't even sure she heard me, but I couldn't waste any more time or Trip was going to hurt my wolf. Pushing through the crowd, I finally broke into the smoky barn and stopped a few feet inside just as Trip ran for the exit.

Trip took one look at me and stopped dead. He stood in the doorway of the smoking barn and wrapped his fingers tightly around my wolf's throat until she couldn't breathe.

"It's you," he growled.

Bastard.

Without another thought, I yanked my cuffs off and threw my hands outward. An unseen force slammed into him, flinging him backward into the burning barn. My wolf went down with him and I surged forward, past the panicked people and animals. My wolf went spectral and wriggled free of Trip's grasp as he attempted to stand up, and then she bolted toward me.

'*Run!*' she said.

I didn't need to be told twice. Pivoting where I stood, I kept my cuffs in my hands and took off at vampire speed with my wolf hot on my heels. I blasted past the scared animals and screaming fey, troll and Ithaki, and caught up with Sage in no time. With a giant leap, my wolf sucked back into my body and I snapped the cuffs on.

"I almost shot you!" Sage grumbled as I appeared quickly at her side. Reaching out, she extended her arm and then pulled me up onto the moving horse carriage.

"Where the hell is Marmal? Did she get away?" Sage peered behind us at the smoking barn that was now in the distance. So she hadn't heard my order to follow them.

I grinned and pointed up to the sky.

Sage looked upward at the shiny white dragon with a tiny brown dot on its back and her mouth popped open. "So...it *can* fly..." she said.

I grinned. "Yep."

Jumping over to my horse, I took the reins and we urged them to go faster. The ride was rough, the carriage bulky, and Trip was no doubt not going to stop looking for us. I chewed on my lip. "If Pearl can carry Marmal all the way to Magic City Prison, we don't need the carriage," I told Sage.

She nodded. "I agree. Cut it loose. We'll go faster without it."

Without another word, I went to work cutting the ropes that tied the carriage to the horses' saddles. We had to slow them so that they didn't get hurt, but I made quick work of it.

"Ready?" I asked.

Sage gripped her horse's reins tightly and I hacked

the last rope loose on either side, seconds apart. It swayed left, since I cut that rope first, and then right, before finally crashing to the ground. Our mares picked up speed then, and I almost fell off with the sudden haste. Clinging to my mare with my thighs, we burst forward with double the speed and set off for Light Fey City.

'Sawyer, I'm almost there. Are you still okay? You're not answering me.' I knew it was probably pointless, but I had to try.

I was beyond relieved when he answered. *'Sorry, love. I got thrown in solitary for the day.'*

My stomach turned to knots at that. *'Why? What happened?'*

'Got in a fight. Someone jumped my roommate. Had to help him out.'

I'm one day away from breaking my felon hubby out of jail and he's getting into fights! *'Well, I wish you weren't fighting, but that's good that you protected Walsh,'* I sent back.

He bristled between our bond and I could feel pain in my shoulder and under my left eye for a moment before he sucked it all back into himself. *'No, love. My roommate isn't Walsh. They would never let us room together. It's Luka...a vampire.'*

I froze, clutching the horse tightly. *'You went to solitary for a vampire?'*

Sawyer sighed inside of my head and I kicked myself

for starting a damn fight when we had such little time to talk.

'He's not like the others. He's saved my butt more times than I can count over the last year. I need you to trust me. He's family.'

Family! Geez. A vampire and Sawyer becoming besties? That was...weird. I blew air through my teeth. 'Okay, I trust you. Is there anything else you can tell me that would help me get you out of there? Like how far is Walsh's cell from yours? What floor are you on? What's your schedule?'

'Walsh is on the same floor as me, eighty, the top one. He's in cell fifty-seven. I'm in cell sixty. We eat lunch together and work out together every day.'

Relief ran through me at that information. That was something I could work with. 'They let you work out? When? Where?' An idea hatched in my mind as I tried to remember what the map of the eightieth floor looked like. Seam said all the cell block floors were laid out the same.

'For one hour a day. No weights, just running, basketball, and other non-lethal things. Four p.m. sharp, before dinner at five. It's a training room on the same floor. We don't leave the top floor. Ever.'

Unless you get thrown in solitary, I wanted to say, but thought better of it.

'How many people work out together?' It would be riskier to break into a room with a bigger group, but probably easier than getting both Walsh and Sawyer out of two separate cells.

I could physically feel him getting further away, like a radio signal going out.

'There are ten guys in my four p.m. workout cohort and ten armed guards.'

Damn. That was a lot of guards for ten men in cuffs that rendered their magic useless.

'Okay. I'll try to aim to get you guys out then, so that—'

'Babe,' Sawyer interrupted me, and I could feel his agony tighten in *my* chest through our bond. *'If anything happened to you while trying to get me out...I could never live with myself. I'm on the top floor. Even if we do get out, how will we get down and across the river and—'*

His concerns were valid. I think a year in that place had made him lose hope, but I don't think he understood that I wasn't going to stop until he was with me, consequences be damned. How could I look my son in the eye when he was older and tell him I let his father be beheaded?

I couldn't.

'Fragile like a bomb, Sawyer, remember?' I reminded him of his own words and what they had meant to me. Everyone underestimated me, Rab, Arrow, even Sawyer. In fact, I think the only person who didn't underestimate me was Astra. I was going to show everyone just what

I was capable of. I was going to finally go off, like a bomb.

'Also, I have a flying dragon,' I added.

His shock ripped through our imprint and filled me up so quickly that I gasped. It felt so good to feel him like that, but with it came a darkness, pain, depression, anger, desperation, love, devotion. So many things he'd been keeping from me.

'A dra—'

His words cut off mid-sentence and then all of his energy was sucked away from me, leaving me feeling like I had a gaping hole in my chest. I clutched the base of my throat, gasping at the sudden loss of him. Tears slipped from the corner of my eyes and I swallowed down the sobs that wanted to rip free.

"You okay?" Sage yelled over the sounds of thundering hooves.

I wiped my eyes and nodded, tightening my grip on the reins and pushing my conversation with Sawyer from my mind as best I could. "Let's ride fast and hard until the Light Fey border. Once we get over, they will stop following us." I looked behind me at the blurs in the distance. Hopefully, Trip didn't have any other animals that could ride faster than a horse. We had a decent lead, so if he was following, we should still outrun them. I'd heard rumors of the dark fey binding animals to them like a shifter would have a wolf. Marmal had confirmed this and more.

Sage pushed her mare harder, then I did the same. My eyes flicked to the sky and spotted the white blur that was Pearl and Marmal. They were tracking us above. We just needed to get to Light Fey City, steal a car, and then make it to the harbor without being spotted.

Easier said than done.

CHAPTER SIX

WE RODE QUICKLY FOR NEARLY AN HOUR, MY BUTT slamming into the hard leather saddle of the horse with each trot. As the border of Light Fey City came up in the distance, we finally slowed.

"Whoa, whoa," I called to my mare and pulled back on her reins. She slowed, her nostrils flaring as she sucked in more air from the rigorous sprint.

"Thanks, girl. You did good." I patted her neck as she pulled to a full stop. Sage and I dismounted swiftly and pulled the packs off the horses. After giving them some of our water, I felt the internal tug of moral obligation.

"What do we do with them?" I asked Sage. They were Paladin horses, horses we probably couldn't spare.

Sage looked up at the sky to see Marmal circling with Pearl.

"Just let them loose? Maybe Rab can send someone

to try to intercept them. Horses are good about finding their way home."

Yeah, but how good? We'd crossed a lot of ground. Maybe if they ran along the border wall and straight into the Wild Lands, through the Ithaki tree houses, they could make it back quicker...

I nodded to Sage, stroking my horse once more. "Go back home, baby," I whispered to her, and aimed her along the stone wall that bordered the two lands. If she ran the length of it, she would hit the Wild Lands. I just hoped she could sense my meaning, if not my words. With a light pat, I swatted her rump and she took off, the other mare right behind her.

'Rab, I'm heading into Light Fey City. Might not talk for a while until I get Sawyer back. I've set the horses free. I'm hoping they will run the length of the border and end up in Wild Lands at Dark Fey border.'

He didn't respond right away and my heart pounded frantically in my chest as my mind spun with all of the reasons why. I was just about to call on Arrow, or Willow, when Rab spoke.

'Okay. I'll send a scout to retrieve them.'

Sage tugged my arm. "We are out in the open. We need to get cover."

I jogged after her, nearly tripping over a bush as Rab's delayed answer spun in my mind. *'What's wrong?'* I finally asked.

He paused again. *'Nothing I can't handle.'*

'*Rab. It's my pack. What's. Wrong?*' I growled and Sage spun to stare at me as I shot her an apologetic look and tapped my forehead. She rolled her eyes, well aware that I was speaking in my head. I didn't like the feeling that I was being kept out of the loop on my own pack.

Rab sighed. '*The Independent Society of Douchebag Wolves, or whatever the hell they call themselves, left the bunker and are trying to find our land. In doing so, they might have tipped off the vampires.*'

Those *idiots!* I knew the second I met that dude that he'd be a problem for us. Probably ran out of food and realized he'd made a mistake. As much as I wanted to wash my hands of it and say it wasn't my problem, they were Sawyer's wolves; until my husband was out of prison, they were my problem.

'*Where are they now?*' I asked.

'*Roaming Ithaki land looking for us in broad daylight like a bunch of buffoons.*'

I threw my arms up in frustration as Sage and I ducked behind a large oak tree right at the border of Light Fey City.

'*Wait until nightfall and then send out a small team to bring them in,*' I told Rab. '*Then double the patrols. If vampires come sniffing around...*' I paused. Do... what? Run? Fight? I wanted to be there with them to make these decisions. '*Try to have the witches shield the place better, but fight to protect what is ours,*' I finally said. I hoped it wouldn't come to any of that.

'*You got it, Alpha. I don't think they will come all the way here. Rumor is Ithaki are on the outs with the vamps for lack of holding up their end of the deal or something.*'

That was a relief. Maybe we could use that to our advantage. I turned to tell Sage what had happened, when a blur streaked behind her in the trees.

"Run!" I shouted at the same time that someone reached around and grabbed me from behind. A strong hand wrapped around my throat and another around my stomach as I was yanked backward and pinned up against someone. Sage moved to help me, when another person leapt out from behind a tree, jerking her backward by the strap of her pack.

My gaze flicked upward into the eyes of Sage's captor and I froze.

Trip was covered in soot from the barn fire. Black ash covered his face and clothing, except for the wrinkled creases on his forehead. He pointed Sage's handgun right at my best friend, as a terrifying look came over his face.

Damn.

My cuffs were on, so I wasn't going to be of much help until I could get them off. Especially if the person holding me was a troll-fey Ithaki, which I guessed they were.

"You. Little. *Hags*," Trip seethed, holding the edge of the gun up to Sage's chin. "You burned down my business. You took my dragon. I'm going to shoot her and make you watch before turning you into the vampires for my very well-earned reward," he growled.

I gulped, trying to assess many things at once. Would he pull the trigger on Sage by the time I could crack the guy holding me in the face? Maybe if I just lunged forward, he would loosen his grip on Sage and direct his attention to me, which would allow her to get away...?

As I was thinking of all these scenarios, Trip and Sage were suddenly covered in a large shadow. It fell over them like...

I grinned, and a millisecond later Pearl swooped from the sky and dug her claws into Trip's back. An ear-splitting yelp ripped from his throat as Sage pulled her head to the side and Trip dropped the gun. He was yanked up into the air by Pearl as the hand around my throat tightened. Sage dove for the gun and I bucked backward with all my strength to dislodge the bastard behind me.

"Not so fast," he growled, doubling down on his grip until black spots danced at the edges of my vision. Why did men always go for the throat? I tried to suck in air, to no avail. I used elbows, heels, nothing worked. He was a giant and I was stuck. My wolf rattled my insides as I started to panic. After everything I'd been through, was I really going to get choked out by a troll? I blinked, no longer having eyes on Sage. Where was my bestie when I needed h—?

The loud bang of a gun ripped through the space and the pressure on my neck released. I fell to the ground with a thud, gasping and sputtering for air. My throat felt like there was a hard ball lodged in the center as I struggled to calm myself. When I'd finally gotten enough oxygen to my brain, I looked to the side and saw Sage holding the gun at her side. She'd shot the troll-fey right in the rib cage, which probably had ripped through his heart so that the bullet wouldn't go into me.

"Couldn't get a clean shot of his head," she said, reaching out a hand to lift me up.

With a sigh of relief, I took her offered hand and stood. "Thank you." I rubbed my throat and looked up at the sky.

Pearl had Trip in her claws while Marmal rode on her back. He was flailing and bucking his arms and legs, trying to dislodge himself. Then suddenly, she just let him go. Trip's scream ripped through the sky and became louder the closer he got. His body dropped like a stone to the ground, and I winced when the hard smack echoed throughout the trees.

"I have a feeling Pearl is going to be helpful," Sage told me. I nodded.

I hated that I couldn't speak into Sage's mind like my other pack members. Marmal too.

An idea formed in my mind and I mulled it over. "Sage can you make non-wolves...pack members?"

Sage's eyes bugged a little, but she nodded. "There are rumors, but...why?" Then her gaze flicked to the sky as Pearl and Marmal flew in slow, wide circles, and landed before us. Pearl stomped the ground with one talon, which was covered in Trip's blood.

Marmal's hair was windswept as she held on to two horns that protruded from Pearl's head.

"Well, she can fly!" I shouted to Marmal as Sage and I stepped closer to them.

Marmal grinned and the small tusks in her cheeks dipped inward. "She can."

"You can speak to her?" I confirmed for the second time, and Marmal simply nodded. Troll magic. Mysterious.

"Tell her thank you. From both of us." I motioned to Sage.

Sage nodded and then looked behind me. "People will have heard all that. We should scram."

She was right. A gunshot and Trip's fall...Light Fey City would be on us in no time. Dark Fey too no doubt.

"Okay, we will steal a car and—"

Marmal shook her head. "Pearl says she can carry up to twenty grown men. You two will feel like feathers."

Ride a dragon! I mean, that was my escape plan after busting Sawyer and Walsh out of prison, but...

"What if we're spotted? I was able to see her clearly the whole time," I argued with my friend.

Marmal nodded. "We wanted you to be able to

83

follow us. She can cloak herself. Old magic. We'll be invisible."

Invisible!

My eyes widened.

'*Is that so crazy?*' my wolf asked.

Touché.

I mean…she could go invisible and walk through walls. Maybe that's where it came from…this old magic.

I looked at Pearl in a new light. Were the dragon and my wolf similar in some way? At least magically?

"Sounds good to me." Sage leapt across the space and Marmal helped her onto the beautiful white dragon.

"Thanks, girl." I reached out to Pearl and stroked her white scales. They felt like a cross between a lizard and a dolphin. Shiny and firm, but soft in a way. It was hard to describe. Her eyes were slitted and the color of the ocean, blue and black and white all mixed into one shiny jewel. Reaching back with her face, she nuzzled my leg and inhaled, her nostrils flaring.

"She says you smell like home," Marmal translated, sounding a bit confused.

I frowned, unsure what that meant. "Where's home?"

Marmal pulled me up and I snuggled in behind Sage, grabbing Pearl's body beneath my legs to steady myself.

Marmal's eyes widened. "She said you would call it the Dark Woods?"

I felt Sage stiffen against me. Pearl was…from the Dark Woods? I thought of the magical cave inside of the mountain and the way the trees moved. If any place in all of Magic City were home to a dragon, it would be there.

Holy crap.

My mind reeled at that revelation, but before I could ponder on it more, Pearl snapped her wings outward.

"Ready?" Marmal asked.

Sage and I had barely said yes when Pearl kicked off the ground and then we were flying. Her giant wings pumped the air as we soared higher and higher. The wind rushed past me, tossing my hair around my face.

"Wooooo!" Sage cried out, but I shushed her with a light elbow to the ribs.

"Fey could be tracking us," I murmured behind her.

"Buzzkill," she grumbled at me.

I looked out at the giant expanse before me and gasped. *Wow.* It was so beautiful up here. You could see the little brick walls demarcating the territories like spokes on a wheel. It was sad, actually, that everyone was so segregated. Because I could see how all of Magic City, as a whole, was so incredibly beautiful. The lands ranged from rich, thick, green forests to the open plains of Troll Village, which were burnt orange and yellow.

Pearl flew over Light Fey City with its black asphalt roads and glass buildings topped with solar panels, and a powerful magic came over us. I could smell the scent of burnt wires as she pulled up some type of shield. It was like I was looking through a plastic bag. Clear, but hazy.

"Okay, she says we are invisible! She's got the cloak up," Marmal screamed behind her at Sage and I.

Okay, *that* was going to be super freaking useful in getting Sawyer out of prison. But I knew the key to having this really go off without a hitch was to be able to communicate with both Sage and Marmal mentally.

"Girls!" I shouted, and they both spun around to face me.

I swallowed hard, and tried to convey the seriousness I felt stirring inside of me. "I want to make you both pack. Paladin pack. My pack. I'll claim you, and that way we can talk into each other's minds..."

Both of their mouths popped open at the same time. "But I'm a troll." Marmal sounded as if she was in complete disbelief.

I nodded. "And you would be accepted as family. Cherished. Loved. Protected." I knew that if I approved it, Rab and the others would as well.

Her eyes grew misty and she nodded. Then I looked at Sage, prepared to put up a fight, prepared to tell her she wasn't really leaving the city wolves behind, she was just joining a blended family.

"I've been pack with you for a while now, Demi. Let's make it official." Sage extended her wrist, knowing what was required, knowing what I'd done to claim Astra.

I inclined my head, tears filling my eyes as I thought of how much I'd been through with this girl.

Reaching out, I removed my left wrist cuff and felt my teeth lengthen, then I dipped my head down to her forearm and nipped her, until I tasted blood.

'*Mine. Pack.*' My wolf surged forward as my alpha power blanketed Sage. I felt our bond deepen as a surge of consciousness joined mine and I sensed Sage so strongly, her worry for me and Walsh and Sawyer, her protective-ness, loyalty. Then she faded into the background with the rest of the pack.

'*Testing, testing,*' I tried.

She grinned. '*That's cool. I've never done that without being in wolf form.*'

A smile pulled at my lips. '*Welcome to the pack.*'

Marmal was next. She extended her arm timidly; she didn't know me as well as Sage did, and she sure as hell didn't know wolf ways, yet still she trusted me. After drawing blood, I claimed her and her conscious-ness surged with mine. There was a frantic panic in her energy and her eyes widened.

She clutched her chest. "I *feel* you."

I nodded. '*I feel you too. You're family now. Pack,*' I finished with a smile, slipping the cuff back on my wrist.

Her mouth opened and closed a few times, like a fish out of water, and then a single tear slipped from her eye. I shouldn't have pressed her but I did; I pushed into her emotions just a tiny bit to see what was wrong, and then tears were lining my eyes as well.

She wasn't alone anymore. Her sister had died in the farm fires last year, and she hadn't realized how lonely she was until this moment that she felt our bond.

I reached out and pulled her in for a hug, in which Sage had to lean over and clutch on to Pearl and out of our way.

'*You're with us now,*' I told her.

'*Happy to be so,*' she responded.

We all flew in reflective silence for the next twenty minutes when the cluster of buildings signaling downtown Magic City, the capital of Light Fey City, rose up into view.

It was stunning. A giant river ran right down the center of the city, spanned by a huge bridge so that cars could go to each side. The river was almost like a lake it was so wide. As we flew closer, I noticed there in the very center of the wide rushing river was the tallest building in the entire city.

Magic City Prison.

There was probably a hundred feet of water on either side of the island, with boat docks and canoes moored on the shores. The city bustled around the island prison as if it didn't exist, cars zipping in and out of traffic, fey walking and laughing as they dressed in their finest suits. It was like a magical Manhattan.

'*Have her set down over there. We need to go over the game plan,*' I told Marmal, pointing to the thick trees that butted up against the river's edge. It looked like some type of parking or hiking trail. It was like they'd cut a city right out of the forest but kept as much nature as possible. I'd never seen so many fey in one place. There were very few in my time at Delphi and they kept to themselves. The way they walked, so lithe and graceful, was almost hypnotic.

Pearl lowered us onto a grassy patch deep within the park, and I dismounted as I stepped out of her invisible shield. We were alone for now, but I pulled the hood up high over my head to cover myself just in case, and then checked that my cuffs were securely on my wrists. Sage and Marmal met me in the grassy area as I paced tracks into the lush blades of green.

I'd made it. I was here. And I had no idea what part of the plan to start next. But looking up at the huge building and knowing my mate was so close gave me hope. I needed to get Sage inside, but getting her arrested now seemed like a big and timely fanfare. There would be sentencing and all of that if it was anything like the jails in Spokane and the human world. My wolf felt on edge as she slithered restlessly inside of me. Were there vampires inside the prison right now? Maybe they lay in wait in these very bushes.

"Tell her to keep cloaked until I figure this out." I pointed to the direction that I knew Pearl was, but instead of a dragon there was just a shimmering bubble not noticeable to the untrained eye.

Marmal nodded. "She will."

"Okay..." I said, not slowing my pacing. "What time is it here?"

Sage pulled a cell phone out of her pocket and turned it on. Holy hell, I hadn't seen one of those in over a year. My fingers itched to check my Instagram account, as silly as that sounded.

"Eugene gave it to me," Sage offered. "It's two p.m. Light Fey time."

Two hours. I had two hours to get Sage inside for a four p.m. jailbreak during Sawyer's workout time, or I'd have to wait another day. I was *not* waiting another day to see my man.

"Okay. I have a plan." I set down my pack and pulled out all the maps.

The workout room on the eightieth floor was directly across from the mess hall and next to the showers on the west side of the building.

"Sage, if you can merge with my wolf and get her inside, she can get up to the eightieth floor to save Sawyer and then come back for you," I told my bestie, knowing it was such a huge ask. She'd be putting her life in danger. If I knew they wouldn't recognize me right away, I'd do it myself. She had already agreed, but I wanted to give her one last chance to back out.

"You know I'm down, but how can I get arrested and sent to prison in two hours?" she asked.

I chewed my lip, an idea forming in my mind. "We're going to test your acting skills."

She frowned and I pointed to Marmal. "You're my getaway car. We will keep Pearl hidden, and then when I direct you, I need you to drop me off at the top floor while we grab the guys, and then we'll go pick up Sage."

Sage raised an eyebrow. "And how am I getting in?"

I sighed. "I need you to pretend to be maintenance. Walk right in the front door and act like you know the place and something is broken. Just enough to get my wolf inside."

Sage shook her head, half smirking. "I have no tools. They won't buy it. But I can probably bull crap long enough to get your wolf in. You and Sawyer owe me the *nicest* possible vacation ever after all this."

I grinned. "Done."

"Okay, I can do this." A shadow crossed her face and she pulled her lower lip into her mouth to chew on it nervously.

"What?" I asked, stepping forward. It was normal to be nervous before something like this. "If I could go myself, I would. I—"

She shook her head. "I wonder what Walsh is like now...?"

Oh.

I'd been able to talk to Sawyer mentally. The last time she had spoken to Walsh, they had ended on a bad note, with him rejecting her for his duty.

"I'm sure they're both different. Sawyer has befriended a vampire," I growled.

Sage scrunched up her face like she smelled something awful. "Really? Gross."

I nodded. "But he'll still be Walsh. *Our* Walsh. Don't worry." I gave her a side hug and she bobbed her head in agreement.

"Question..." Marmal held up a hand. "There are magical wards all over that place." She pointed to the building. "We won't be able to fly close enough unless we bring it down. And didn't you say the boys are wearing cuffs that electrocute them if they step foot off the premises? How are you going to deal with all that? We don't have a witch and I can't bring them down."

Damn. She was right, and she'd also given me another clue into her magic. She could see wards. I should have brought Raven or Star, but maybe Marmal was good enough. I hadn't known then all that would be involved, and I had wanted to protect them by leaving them behind.

I planned on stealing a key to get the boys' cuffs off, but the other magical wards...I had no plan for. Were they like the cuffs? Because I'd gotten my cuffs off once...it took a fey blade and some blood but—

"Do light fey carry fey blades? Or is that only a dark fey thing?" I asked.

Marmal's eyes widened a little. "*All* fey carry their birth blade. It's a big deal to their culture."

Okay...okay...

I paced harder. I had two hours. I would need my

attention to be with my wolf and Sage, but maybe I could sneak away and steal a fey blade before—

"I'll do it." Marmal stepped forward and pulled a small dagger from behind her back. She gripped it in a tight fist and looked at me with determination.

"Do what?" I hadn't said anything yet.

"You want a fey blade, right? But you need to stick with Sage since your wolf will be with her? I'll get it and meet you back here before four p.m." Marmal crossed a fist over her chest.

Wow, how had I lucked out with such supportive women by my side?

"Thank you," I croaked.

She nodded and looked back in the direction of Pearl, probably communicating mentally.

'I'll keep in touch.' She tapped her head and pushed the words into my mind. I gave her a half-cocked grin.

Marmal was pack, and I felt so right with that decision. After our troll pack member slunk away into the hiking trail to rob some unsuspecting fey of their blade, I turned to Sage.

Placing one hand on either of her shoulders, I looked her right in the eyes and took a deep breath.

"Are you ready for my wolf to...join you?"

She swallowed hard. "Nope. Totally freaked out, have already imagined the worst, like she gets stuck, or I throw up, or lose my mind...but let's do this."

I couldn't help but laugh. "Oh, girl, I love you."

She grinned. "Just don't get stuck. I like having only one soul in my body."

I gave her a curt nod, as if I knew what I was doing when in fact I was scared myself. I didn't want half of my soul stuck in another person's body either! My wolf was ready, perched just at the edge of my skin, blocked only by the magic of the cuffs Sawyer had custom-made for me.

Reaching out, I pulled them off but kept them in my hands, ready to put them back on the second my wolf came out. Sending my scent, or whatever, out into Light Fey City, was not something I wanted to do right now.

The moment my wolf leapt from my body and onto the grass before me, I snapped the cuffs back on. My wolf was still spectral, not yet solidifying her body as she looked from Sage to me.

'It's going to be weird, I know,' I told her. *'But we gotta do it to get Sawyer.'*

Sage balled her hands to fists and braced herself like she was preparing to be hit, then her eyes flashed yellow.

'Her wolf doesn't like it,' my wolf said.

I shrugged. *'Tough. She'll get over it.'* I was in alpha mode now and I was bringing my baby daddy home today no matter what.

My wolf nodded, and then leapt.

It was like time stopped. My wolf arced through the air as Sage flinched, closing her eyes and holding her breath. I held mine too, and so did my wolf. No one breathed, the wind didn't blow, it was like the world stopped for a moment just to witness half of my soul merging with another person. Then she disappeared. She leapt right into Sage's chest and…she was gone. A shock ripped through me, like electricity zapping up my spine. I cried out at the same time Sage did, our tandem screams ripping through the forest.

It hurt, like my skin was on fire, but only for a second before it was gone. *'What the hell was that?'* I asked my wolf.

'Her wolf fought me for a second before relenting,' she told me.

Sage panted, holding her chest and looking over at me with wide eyes. "This is the *weirdest* feeling of my life and I want it to stop as soon as possible."

I winced, feeling Sage's discomfort through our bond. It was bad for me too, but not as much as her.

"Sorry. Let's do this quickly then." I called her over to the edge of the river. We walked around the shimmering transparent bubble that was Pearl's cloak and I knelt down at the edge of the water. Reaching into the thick wet mud, I dabbed a small amount on my finger and dragged some across Sage's neck and cheeks before rubbing it in with my palm to make it look like engine grease.

She stepped away from me. "What the heck?"

I rolled my eyes. "You have to look like a mechanic who works on AC units or something. Right now you look like a sexy, redheaded Lara Croft Tomb Raider."

Sage frowned. "Who?"

95

I shook my head. "We are overdue for a movie night, my friend."

She closed her eyes, relenting, and stepped closer to me as I rubbed the mud on her clothes.

"I actually hate you right now, and Sawyer owes me so big. I want a red Range Rover with white leather seats when I get home," Sage growled.

I grinned as I started to tease her hair a little, making it look wild like she'd been working under the hood of a car all day. "You got it, babe. And a house with a view. Whatever you want."

We both knew we were half kidding. Who knew when that type of life would come back into normalcy. But if it didn't, I'd get her a white horse and cottage on Paladin land, whatever she wanted that I was capable of giving.

"All right, let's do a practice. You have to seem like you know mechanical stuff."

She nodded sticking one hand in the front of her pants and scratching her stomach. "I heard you gotta AC problem. Probably the carburetor. When those regulators get overheated, they need quick attention before they go boom."

I bit down on my lips to keep from bursting into laughter. "That's perfect. Go try to get in but be harmless, you don't want them to magically cuff you before my wolf can get out."

She nodded, looking at the water. Across the river

about a hundred feet was the giant prison, all glass but tinted so dark I couldn't see anything. A thirty-foot fence dotted the perimeter with glowing blue barbwire. It was definitely magic.

I'd cross that bridge when I got to it.

"Be safe, okay? I want Sawyer back, but not at the expense of losing you. If it goes sideways, get out," I told her.

She nodded, but we both knew that was easier said than done.

She moved to jump into the water and I rushed forward, pulling her into a hug. "I love you, Sage Hudson. Like big, huge love. You're my sister no matter that our DNA says different." My voice cracked and I wanted to kick myself for getting all emotional, but if anything happened to this woman, I needed her to know how much she meant to me.

Pulling back, she wiped her teary eyes, smearing mud deeper into her cheeks. "I love you too. That's why I'll go to the grave with the knowledge that when you delivered Creek, you pooped all over my hand." She grinned.

My mouth popped open at that declaration. "Shut the hell up. That's not true."

She just raised one eyebrow and then waltzed into the water.

What the hell?

"Sage!" I whisper-screamed. "Is that true?" Because that was mortifying.

My bestie just chuckled before stepping into the water and wading across.

There was *no way* I pooped on her hand. Totally no way...right?

Pushing that revelation from my mind, I slunk into the bushes and watched as Sage waded across the river. Anxiety ramped up inside of me as she inched her way across, going farther and farther away from me. As she neared the shore on the other side, she stood up out of the water and started to yell to one of the guards.

Okay, the acting had begun.

I shifted my perspective to my wolf and immediately wanted to recoil. It was...a tight fit being inside of Sage. Her wolf kept pushing against mine and it made it feel claustrophobic in a way that was hard to describe. Sage reached the sandbank and started wave her arms.

"Your main gate is broken!" she shouted up at a guard tower that sat high above the giant fence. "I'm here to fix the AC!" she screamed.

"Stop right there!" someone bellowed, and a red laser beam from the scope of a gun appeared on Sage's chest. She looked up at the giant fence and the fey now standing on top of it. He peered down at her with scrutiny, rifle raised.

"I'm here to fix the AC, jerk!" Sage screamed. "Your main gate is broken so I had to walk. Let me in before I get your stupid butt fired!"

Holy smokes, she really was going to deserve an Oscar for this.

The fey man frowned, lowering his scope. "You're trespassing. Violators are shot on sight."

Sage shrugged. "Okay. It's your job not mine." Then she started to walk away.

"Damn." The dude looked over his shoulder and spoke to a second dude, barely visible from this angle. "Fine, let her in so we can verify she's actually here to fix something."

Sage smiled and turned back around to face the guy. I could see from my spot across the river that the wall above her started to move. A stone gate was hidden in the wall so that you couldn't see it until it was retracting to gain entry. The brick pattern was a cream speckled barrage of muted colors so that even the gate's hinges were camouflaged.

Two guards waltzed out, guns raised at Sage as she raised her hands in a gesture of peace.

The two guards looked down at her with a glare, their pointy fey ears peeking out from the sides of their black baseball caps, and I moved closer inside of the bushes where I was hiding to get a better look. A hundred feet was far when you had to swim that length, but so close when you were hiding in a bush trying to avoid being seen.

"Where're your tools?" one asked her, gun pointed at her chest.

"In my car down the road at your broken gate, which I'll probably also have to fix," she shot back.

One of them inhaled. "She's a wolf? What the hell is a wolf doing all the way out here to fix the AC?" I was seeing through my human eyes but hearing what they were saying through my wolf, who was in Sage. It was a weird out-of-body sensation.

"My boyfriend is fey. I like my ears pointy." She puckered her lips.

Four other guards came out now, aiming their guns into the trees across the riverbank, right at me, and I slunk backward fully so that I could no longer see them from my human body.

My heart pounded in my chest as I used my wolf's hearing to listen to what the men said.

"She's got to be kidding us," one of the guards said.

"Let's get her inside and ask the warden what he wants to do about it," another said.

"Rules state we shoot all violators on sight. This smells of an ambush to me," a new, cold male voice called out and raised his gun, aiming it at her chest.

I flinched, just as one of the other males stepped in front of the gun. "On the off chance she is who she says she is…" He paused and the guy lowered his weapon.

"Fine. Bring her to the warden," he growled. "But if she so much as lunges as you, kill her." Then he stooped down and pulled a roll of duct tape from his cargo pants.

In one quick motion he ripped a piece off and taped it over her mouth.

Sage didn't move a muscle. The guard pulled her hands behind her back and walked her inside. Excitement thrummed through me. It was happening.

The prison break was a go.

CHAPTER SEVEN

S AWYER, *I'M HERE,*' I PUSHED OUT TO HIM. 'CAN YOU *hear me?*'

I paced the small grove tucked just inside the thick wall of bushes, but no response came.

Sage had been moved to some type of medical room. After they realized she had no ID and maintenance was not called, she faked a seizure. Marmal was still stalking a fey jogger.

When Sawyer didn't say anything after a long moment, I snapped my attention back to Sage. They had her strapped to a medical bed, and she bucked against the restraints as a fey doctor walked in wearing a white lab coat. The room was on the bottom floor, and Sage's bed was right in front of a window with pale yellow curtains. The room was actually nice, clean and modern. I was surprised.

"She was found swimming in the river, and then she had what appeared to be a seizure," a young male assistant said to the doctor, handing her a clipboard.

Sage snapped her head to the female doctor fey, who had long flowing red hair like hers. "The flies are in the universe to my pots and pans!" Sage said urgently.

The doctor frowned. "She may have recently had a stroke. This sounds like word salad."

Word salad? Was that a medical term? Good thinking, Sage. My bestie was smart and she must have known the symptoms.

"Let's sedate her for transport." The doctor signed something on the clipboard and handed it back. Then she held out her hand and the assistant plopped a long syringe into her palm, the needle reflecting the light from the ceiling.

Fear spiked through Sage and I knew it was now or never with my wolf.

'I *won't leave this place without you. I would die before that happened, you have to believe me,*' I told Sage.

'I *trust you,*' she whimpered.

My wolf leapt free of Sage's chest then, but at the same time, she went invisible, activating whatever power Pearl also used, *old magic.*

"Don't make the sleep come. Lizards are peonies," Sage whimpered to the doctor, keeping up the act.

The doctor frowned. "Poor girl. Might have been out in the heat too long. She'll need a full workup. I thought the wolves all died in the war or went underground or something?" she asked her assistant, a black-haired male fey with freckles.

He shrugged. "Maybe she's a refugee."

The doctor put the needle to Sage's arm and I felt my bestie's panic shoot through our pack bond. My wolf was hiding in the corner, waiting to see what would happen to Sage before she started trying to find Sawyer. If they were going to hurt her, we were out of here, and I'd have to find another way to get my man out.

"I like the wolves. They were once our strongest ally before Prime Minister Locke ruined that," the doctor stated.

I nearly sagged with relief. They wouldn't hurt Sage.

'You'll be okay. I'll come right back for you,' I told Sage.

'Okay...' was all she muttered, and then the doctor plunged the needle into her arm and the heaviness of drugged sleep took her quickly.

My wolf stayed, watching the doctor and waiting. She wouldn't leave this room without knowing what was going to happen to my bestie, and I was grateful for that. I felt confident they wouldn't hurt her after overhearing their conversation, but she wanted to wait one more minute.

Someone knocked on the door and peeked their head in. "Transfer called. They can't get here until six p.m. for the wolf."

The doctor nodded. "She can sleep it off in here until they come. I can give her another dose at five if she wakes."

Five.

I looked at the clock. It was already three-fifteen. I had less than two hours to get Sawyer out of here and come back for Sage before they drugged her again. As the doctor and nurse left, they locked the room and I took one last look at Sage's sleeping form before my wolf slipped through the wall and into the hallway.

She scanned the hallway, looking for a stairwell, and then started in the direction of a glowing exit sign. I could sense her thoughts. She was thinking that she couldn't get into a crowded area, because although she was invisible, someone with the right magic might see her. And fey had the right magic. They were even more elusive than the trolls. God only knew what they were truly capable of.

I felt Marmal tug at my consciousness and I pulled away from my wolf, trusting her to know how to get to the eightieth floor. When I opened my eyes, Marmal was running toward me, holding her side as blood soaked her shirt. I rushed forward in panic.

'*We need to get on Pearl and take to the skies,*' she told me. '*I'm being chased, but I got the blade.*' She held up a bright silver fey blade and I nodded.

When she reached me, I stared down at her stomach.

'*How bad is it?*' It didn't look like it was actively bleeding anymore, so that was a good sign.

"I'm fine. Let's go!" she whisper-screamed, just as I heard shouts come from the main walking trail.

"I was attacked!" a woman screamed.

Damn.

We both ran straight for where Pearl was resting, and she lowered her shield so that we could step inside. We'd barely made it into the shield that rendered us invisible when a female fey and two armed security guards stepped into the meadow.

"I smell blood," the woman seethed. Without another word, we slipped onto Pearl's back and she kicked off the ground, beating her wings, which caused the bushes and tall grass around us to flatten.

"What was that!?" the woman shrieked, staring at the windstorm Pearl had created. The guards raised their weapons and I flinched, hoping they wouldn't shoot randomly into the air. Pearl climbed higher until they were just a speck in the distance, then I relaxed a little.

"Let me see." I peeled Marmal's hand back and inspected a clean one-inch cut along her rib cage.

"That will need stitches, but it doesn't seem to have hit any major organs," I told her, the guilt of her injury weighing heavily on me. "Let me get the med-kit."

She shooed my hand away. "I'm fine. I've had worse. How's Sage? What's going on inside?"

She handed the fey blade to me and I took it with gratitude. "Thanks for getting that." I then quickly brought her up to speed about how things had gone with Sage as I dug around my pack for the med-kit to tend to her injury best I could while riding on a freaking flying dragon. After cleaning and bandaging her wound as Pearl circled the park area, I tuned into my wolf next.

She was on the forty-fourth floor, panting from going up all the stairs. She couldn't use vampire speed because I had the cuffs on, and I was worried about taking them off. Somehow we were still connected, and even though she could go invisible, she couldn't use some of our other powers. Me wearing the cuffs was draining her it seemed like...

She was worried to try to sneak into an elevator and get stuck going down, or have someone notice her. The stairwell was relatively unmanned but for one janitor she'd passed on floor twenty-six.

It was nearly four p.m. She had fifteen minutes to get to the eightieth floor, but I didn't tell her that. Workout hour was until five, but I needed to get Sage before they came in and gave her another dose of that medication. This was all going to hinge on me being able to actually break through this protection spell and into one of these windows.

Breathe, just breathe.

I reached into Sage's pack and pulled out the sleek black phone she kept there. If anyone could tell me how to break through a fey magic protection, it would be my other bestie. I dialed Raven's number by heart and prayed that her cell phone still worked. Technically, we were somewhere in Idaho, hidden in the Magic Lands, and cell towers definitely worked in Idaho…

"Hello?" she answered tentatively.

"Thank God you still have a phone," I told her.

"Holy crap, Demi," Raven breathed. "I almost didn't pick up. I'm surprised this thing is still connected after a year underground."

I grinned. "It's good to hear from you. I have a problem that needs a magical solution."

"I'm here with Star. Putting you on speaker," Raven announced.

That was good, I would need all hands on deck.

"The Magic City Prison is surrounded by some… bluish electrocuting protection spell. It smells fey in origin. I need to bring it down so I can get close enough to break a window to get the guys out."

"Fey protections are very complex. What do you have to work with?" Star sounded skeptical and it made me nervous.

"Well, we got a fey blade," I told her.

"That's great!" she and Raven said at the same time.

"And I have a dragon."

The phone went silent and I pulled it back to make sure it hadn't died. Nope, still running.

"Hello?" I called out.

"Did you say you have a *dragon*?" Raven shrieked.

"Alive or dead?" Star whispered.

Wow.

"Alive, flying on her back at this moment. Can she help?"

"Can she *help*?" Star sounded offended by my suggestion. "Dragons are the mothers of magic. Holy smokes. Can I meet her? Like once this is all over?" I could hear the excitement in Star's voice.

"Focus," Raven chastised her.

"Sorry. Right. Will she let you peel off one of her scales? If so, I can give you an incantation to coat the fey blade in and it will cut through the protection magic like butter," Star told me.

I looked to Marmal, who was listening intently as I'd also put the phone on speaker. My troll friend was quiet a moment before nodding. "She said you may have one scale so long as the magic it's used for does not hurt another," Marmal translated.

"Ohhh, you have someone who can communicate with her!" Star screeched in exhilaration.

I nodded, then remembered she couldn't see me. "My troll fr—pack member," I amended and Marmal smiled.

"Okay, here's what you need to do." Star then proceeded to tell me the incantation that would break the spell, and after thanking her and Raven, I hung up.

I checked in with my wolf then. She was on the seventy-sixth floor and had stopped, panting against the brick wall. She was tired, thirsty, and ready for a nap. It was all made that much harder by the fact that we weren't together. We drew strength from one another.

'*You got this,*' I told her, trying to give her the encouragement she needed to run up those last three floors.

'*Demi? I feel you near!*' Sawyer's voice boomed through our bond and the sudden joy of it knocked into my chest.

My wolf pushed off the wall, inspired by hearing our mate. His voice coursed through her, giving her the final momentum she needed. When I tried too hard to think of her, or I, or us, it hurt my brain. We were one and she felt what I felt, and I felt what she felt. We both wanted Sawyer, and we wanted to see him right now!

Bursting up the stairs, her legs shook with fatigue and I thought she might collapse as she panted and her lungs burned. Two more floors left.

'*My wolf is on the seventy-eighth floor. Get ready,*' I told Sawyer, peering at the map I'd spread out before me as Marmal pulled the scale from Pearl's flank. It was one that seemed already loose and Pearl didn't flinch, so I felt less bad about taking it.

I instructed Pearl which window to fly over to, which I hoped was the workout room based on what the maps said.

'*I'm walking into the gym room now,*' Sawyer told me. '*Walsh is here. How many of us can you get out? I can't leave without my crew.*'

His crew?

'*How many are in your crew?*'

'*There are five of us, including me and Walsh.*'

Well, that wasn't planned. *'And this vampire friend is one of them?'* I asked sourly.

'Yes, Luka is family to me. I know it's hard for you to understand, Demi, but—'

I didn't want to argue right now. *'It's fine. We can take all five.'*

Pearl said she could carry twenty grown men. We'd have to make it work.

My wolf walked up the last step and her back legs started to shake. She was so fatigued, so tired, and yet she pushed on. Using what little magic she had left, she pushed through the wall and into the eightieth floor cellblock.

And holy shifter was it intimidating. The walls were lined with barred cells, men paced inside, two to a cell. She passed a fey, a troll, a warlock, wolf, Ithaki. They didn't discriminate here; every type of creature was present and locked up. My wolf stared at a fey man who stood behind the bars of his cell. His ankles were bound with silver cuffs similar to the ones I grew up with, scars and angry red skin peeking out just above them, showcasing how many times he'd tried to use his power.

Swiveling her head, my wolf looked out into the open space outside of the cells. The room was a long rectangle and the cells ran to the left, right, and back side of the wall. My wolf peered over her shoulder to see a guard sitting at a desk and scrolling through a tablet. My wolf had zero issues walking through the walls here so far, so that was good. She wouldn't need the handprint of a guard to open the workout room door, but she would need the keys to unlock the cuffs from the guys or they'd all be crispy fried bacon when they tried to leave.

My wolf padded over to the tall, lithe fey guard sitting hunched over his tablet, his ankles crossed, finger poised over the screen as he scrolled through some website. My wolf scanned his body, looking for a set of clunky keys that would hang from his belt like in the movies. There was no such set of keys.

'*Sawyer,*' my wolf whispered through the bond. '*What do the cuff keys look like?*'

My cuffs had always been magically taken off, but that wouldn't work here with so many inmates and the prison run by mostly fey, not witches. They'd need an easier way to remove them when they were damaged and needed to be replaced or whatever.

Sawyer's response was immediate. '*It's a square magnet that hangs from a black cord on their necks. The clasp only releases if the guard touches it. It's some kind of new smart technology that matches their fingerprint.*'

Okay, that sounded complicated, especially for my wolf to manage without hands…

"Wolf!" The guard looked up from his tablet suddenly and hissed. His eyes locked right on my wolf and she froze.

Crap. He saw me. Her. *Us.*

Some fey had that magic, and of course it had to be

this guard! One second my wolf was transparent and the next she solidified, lunging at his neck. His arms came up immediately and latched on to her neck as a shock ran through my wolf. She quivered as his magic rushed through her, trying to weaken her.

No.

Back on Pearl, in my human body, I ripped off the cuffs, power surging from me to my wolf. She yanked out of the guard's grasp with surprising force, dropping to the ground. He reached for a red button on the desk, and that's when she lunged for his crotch, sinking her teeth into the meat between his legs. An inhuman wail cut through the space and the men in the caged cells started to cheer and beat on the bars as they watched it all go down.

The fey dropped to the ground, and a shock wave burst from his body, but my wolf was ready. She saw the change in the air, and as it came for her, she used her vampire-like speed and strength to push through it. With the cuffs off of me now, it was no holds barred. No limit to our power.

His protective force field snapped against her skin with the strength of a bullet and I knew that was going to hurt tomorrow. Wasting no time, she lunged again for his neck, pouncing first on his chest to pin him down. Power pulsed through me to her and she wasted no time lunging at his jugular with her teeth.

His arms came up to yank her off, but it was too

late. His throat came out in one swift jerk; muscle and tendons tore away cleanly. She spit the meat onto the ground as he went limp underneath her. The men in the cells went wild, yelling and banging loudly.

'Guards coming to see what that noise is all about,' Sawyer told my wolf and me.

Damn.

Pouncing off of the dead guard, my wolf went ghostly as she reached over and pulled his wrist gently into her mouth. She stepped awkwardly over his chest and tried to maneuver his limp hand in a way that would press his finger to the clasp around the necklace at his now mangled throat.

Gross.

Using her muzzle, she dug under his neck, rolling his head to the side while his hand was still firmly clenched in her mouth.

'We're going to need therapy after this,' I told my wolf as his blood splashed over her muzzle. I was pleased to see that even invisible, she could still maneuver him.

"HEY!" a guard yelled behind her and my wolf froze. "What's all that racket?" he shouted. My wolf's gaze flicked to the side to see two fey guards had just come out into the main room and were facing the prisoners, who were banging wildly on their cell bars with cups and fists. The guards hadn't looked my way yet, they were too preoccupied with the wild prisoners.

But they would soon.

One of them turned toward my wolf, and a wolf prisoner in the nearest cell shouted, "I'm bleeding!" He clutched his stomach and fell over.

The two fey guards ran to his cell and it dawned on me that he was buying me time.

Thanks, dude.

My wolf resumed the acrobatic nuzzling, trying to get the dead fey guard's finger up to the clasp at the back of his neck. Finally she succeeded and the necklace fell away with a click.

Yes!

Without a moment to waste, she picked the necklace up into her mouth and bolted away from the lifeless guard.

Her eyes scanned doors, grateful that the dude in the cell was having some fake fit to distract the new guards.

Bathroom.

Utility closet.

Gym.

Gotcha.

Walking through the door that said *Gym*, my wolf stopped dead at the sight of Sawyer, and all the breath whooshed out of my human form sitting on Pearl.

Holy hot felon.

My sweet preppy billionaire husband had changed. He now had a full beard and was standing shirtless under the bar where he was doing chin-ups. The muscles in his arms popped as my wolf's gaze ran over the biggest change to Sawyer.

His body was *covered* in tattoos.

RIP Dad was written in cursive above an anatomical heart on his forearm. *Alpha* was written above an image of a howling wolf on his bicep. *Hudson* was in huge block letters across his abs, and then my wolf's gaze flicked to his chest. Right over his heart was my name in a beautiful cursive script.

Demi.

A whine caught in my wolf's throat, and Sawyer's eyes snapped to her.

He'd always been able to see me no matter if I was invisible to others or not. He stilled, and I suddenly became aware of all the other people in the room who *couldn't* see me: eight guards and ten scary looking supernaturals. I almost yipped in joy when I saw Walsh standing behind a male vampire who was punching a speedbag. The vampire's hair was dark black, slicked back with sweat, and holy yum, I hated to admit it but he was insanely hot. All of these dudes were. They were ripped as hell, covered in tattoos and beards and sweating testosterone like it was air. My wolf shook herself to clear her thoughts and padded slowly over to Sawyer. He hadn't moved, just stood frozen as he stared at me.

Sawyer coughed twice, really short, and it must have been some signal, because Walsh, the hot vampire dude, and some fey prisoner all started to move in unison over to Sawyer.

"Hudson! Walsh! Bennett! No congregating," a guard called. My wolf had reached Sawyer, and when he bent down to tie his shoe, she spit the necklace onto the ground at his feet. He grabbed it with shaking fingers just as the vampire—it must be Luka, Sawyer's roommate—started to heckle the guard.

"I pulled my back, man," Luka said as Walsh started to inspect Luka's back.

"Let me see," the fey called out, moving closer as they covered the fact that Sawyer was uncuffing himself.

"I missed you so damn much," Sawyer whispered as he looked right into the eyes of my wolf and unclicked the remaining cuff, putting the glowing blue set, which now stood open, behind a floor mat to hide them. Sawyer ran his fingers through my wolf's fur and I whimpered again. It felt so good to be touched by him, to see him, smell him.

Back on Pearl, I instructed Marmal with a half sob of joy. "It's time."

Back in the room, Sawyer handed the key to Walsh next and started to inspect Luka's back. "Oh damn, is that a bone sticking out?" Sawyer yelled loudly, looking at Luka's perfect, muscled back, covered with tattoos and zero bones sticking out.

"He's a vampire. He'll heal. Break it up!" A fey guard pushed off the wall and walked over to Sawyer, gun raised.

Back on Pearl, I shook myself. Crap was going to go down and we needed to do this, now.

"Fly me as close as you can to that window and be ready to scram the second I get them out!" I yelled to Marmal, who sat in front of me.

She nodded, and directed Pearl over to the far window on the very top floor. There was a tiny ledge, maybe six inches in depth. Nothing I could stand on. The closer Pearl flew to the window, the more I could sense the magic at work in the protective shields. It was like a rainbow sheen of oil or bubbles suspended in the air.

"She can't get any closer or her wing will hit the shield!" Marmal shouted.

Frick. I was a good ten feet away from the shimmering shield. But it was now or never. I was so close to getting Sawyer out and I still had Sage to worry about.

"When I start to fall, catch me!" I shouted. "I'm going to jump and bring down the shield."

I held up the fey blade and Marmal's eyes widened. She was quiet a moment, but then nodded.

I looked down, barely able to see the river, as we were over eight hundred feet in the air.

Please don't let this be how I die, I sent up a silent prayer to whomever might be listening, and then I plunged the fey blade into my palm. A slice of burning pain radiated along my hand as a thick line of crimson blood pooled into my palm and saturated the knife.

I mumbled the incantation that Star had told me, and the knife glowed with a sickly green hue.

Well, that was something at least. I was fully just going to have to trust that this spell worked, and the second I drove the blade into the protective shield...it would break.

"Old magic. I have old magic and that's good, it's going to work," I ranted out loud, trying to psych myself up for this jump.

My wolf pulled on my attention and I snapped my focus to her just in time to see Luka headbutt a security guard in the face, and then Sawyer roundhouse kick another.

Oh damn.

Okay.

Here goes nothing.

"One." I stood on Pearl's back, teetering in the air as she flapped her wings to try to keep me steady. "Two." I gripped the blade tighter in my fist. "Three!" I shouted.

And then I leapt. Out into the air, stabbing with my blade hand into the protective shield, sending a ripple of pain up my elbow. There was a cracking noise...and then I was falling.

Oh damn.

Freefalling from eight hundred feet is probably the most terrifying thing I could ever imagine, and I'd been through some scary crap. Even knowing Pearl would try her best to catch me did nothing to quell my nerves.

'*Demi!*' Sawyer screamed. He must have picked up on my emotions and felt my terror. I ignored him, just focusing on breathing and not passing out when Pearl materialized just beneath me.

"Here!" Marmal shouted and I reached for her. With surprising force, I slammed onto Pearl's back, sending her jerking to the left. Marmal latched on to me, planting both arms onto my shoulders to steady me. We nearly both fell off, but then Pearl was able to right herself.

Reaching out, I stroked her scales. "I'm so sorry if that hurt."

Marmal looked at me with a half-cocked grin. "She said it felt like a deep tissue massage."

I frowned. How the hell did an ancient dragon know what a deep tissue massage was? Shaking my head, I forced myself to focus. "Get me back up there. We might only have minutes before they get the shield back up."

"You got it!" Marmal instructed her and then Pearl flapped her wings maddingly as she careened closer to the building now that the protective shield was gone. As we drew closer and closer, I readied myself for what was likely to be the most painful part of this process. Smashing the window open with my body. From what Sawyer said there was nothing heavy or dangerous inside that could be used as a weapon. No free weights or anything. That left me, hurling through the air like a ball—

"Do you want Pearl to smash the window with her tail?" Marmal suddenly asked, breaking my thoughts.

I looked back at Pearl's tail. At the tip were six knobby horns of various sizes.

Oh...that was a better option. I wanted to facepalm myself but refrained. There was a wild prison fight going on inside and I needed to help.

"Yes please!" I shouted, and seconds later the sound of shattering glass rang through the air.

Sawyer!

I sensed him before I saw him. Looking up from Pearl's back, I pivoted and there he was, standing in front of the broken window, fingers curled deep into my wolf's fur as she stood at his feet. Blood trickled down his neck from a wound at his ear and his chest heaved as he tried to catch his breath. But even still, he gave me a full panty-dropping grin, complete with dimple.

Holy shifter, I'd missed that smile.

"Demi!" he screamed, opening his arms.

I wasted no time. Standing on Pearl's back, I jumped from the dragon in one leap, trying to keep all my crap together so I didn't break down into sobs. It had been so long since I held him, smelled him, *tasted him.* We had a damn baby together and he didn't even know until recently. The second I crashed into his chest, his arms came around me like a vise.

"Holy hell, woman," he rasped as I wrapped my legs around his waist, trying to get closer to him. His breath shuddered against me as I released the sobs I'd been keeping in. He squeezed me so hard it hurt, but I didn't care because on some level it felt good. Being held so tightly against his shirtless body was the best damn feeling I'd had in a long time.

Pulling back from him a little, I looked up into his searing blue eyes and allowed our imprint to fully enmesh once more. I opened myself to him, every emotion, every experience I'd had since we had been apart. Having Creek, becoming Paladin alpha, surviving the Dark Woods, missing him. All of it. He just looked into my eyes and nodded. Then I felt him open. He'd kept so much from me. There was so much darkness in him now, I wasn't prepared for it. He'd contemplated suicide so many times in our absence together. He was beaten daily by guards and other rival prison gangs. He'd been starved, electrocuted thousands of time, near death. My chest felt like a five-hundred-pound weight sat on it as he pushed his emotions into me, sharing all he'd been through. He almost lost his mind not knowing what had become of me. The only thing that kept him together and going was his new pack of friends and the hope that I was alive. A tear slipped down my cheek knowing he'd been through so much pain. Leaning forward, he kissed the tear, melting it into his mouth.

"I love you so much," I croaked.

His lips landed on mine and I couldn't breathe for a moment, couldn't move. Was this actually real? Were we finally together? I moaned as his warm wet tongue slipped into my mouth and I tasted him for the first time in forever.

"Hey, lovebirds, a little help!" Walsh suddenly cried.

Shaken from our reunion, Sawyer pulled back from our kiss and set me down, then we both spun.

Crap.

I noticed Luka, Walsh, and two other guys. I was assuming they were the rest of his "crew." One was fey and the other troll. They were all locked into a vicious fight with five guards. Fists pounded, blood flew, bodies cracked, all in an effort to wrestle the guns away from them. The other men in the workout room were in the corner pulling weapons off of the dead fey guards and arming themselves.

Great.

Luka, the vampire, had uncuffed himself, and now tossed a guard across the room as if he were made of paper. The guard hit the wall with a thud just as another fey guard lunged for Luka, blade drawn. Sawyer jumped into the fight and I felt my power surge within me. We needed to get the hell out of here—and we needed to get Sage. That shield could go back up any minute, trapping us all inside of it. I surged forward with vampire speed and slammed into the fey guard about to stab Luka. His body crashed against the wall and I took his head into my hands and twisted. The sickening crunch of his neck breaking rang throughout the room and I dropped him on the floor and turned. Two remaining guards were rushing toward me.

"Demi!" Sawyer screamed, panic in his face. The guards had guns raised.

A pulse of power flared to life under my skin and I flung my arms out, sending a shield of magic at them akin to a bomb blast. It looked like a wave of blue light, and when it slammed into their bodies, they turned to ash.

"Holy crap," Sawyer breathed, looking at the two piles of ash.

Okay, that was freaky. I'd never done that before.

I swallowed hard, a bit shaken, and glanced around the room. The other guards had been killed or subdued.

"Damn, where can I find a woman like that?" Luka appraised me with pride. My gaze ran over his tattoos. **Five Crew** was printed in big block letters across his collarbone. I looked at Sawyer's collarbone. Then Walsh. Then the fey and troll. They all had the same thing. This was Sawyer's pack.

I'd accepted Marmal and Sage as my pack. And this was how Sawyer got through the last year. I wasn't going to be a prick just because I hated vampires.

Sawyer grinned. "I told you she was amazing."

Luka bowed before me, taking my hand into his and lightly kissing the top. "My lady Alpha, I am forever in your debt."

Whoa. Was it hot in here or...? This charmer was

nothing like the cold vampires I had met. I squirmed under his gaze and nodded as he released my hand.

"A friend of Sawyer's is a friend of mine," I told him.

He chuckled. "I know you hate my kind. That's okay. My family is a bunch of douchebags."

"Family?" I asked, cocking my head to the side.

Sawyer cleared his throat. "We should get out of here."

Right.

"I'm Talon," the troll dude said. He was a giant guy, standing well over six feet tall and looked like he was cut out of stone.

"Bennett." The fey male saluted me. "Thanks for the save."

All of the men in Sawyer's little crew were extremely good-looking and I knew Marmal and Sage would have no qualms about spending the next few days with them.

I nodded. "Well met." We walked over to the busted-out window just as an alarm rang throughout the prison.

Sage.

They had finally figured out there was a prison break going on.

"Lockdown procedures commence now. We have an active infiltration," a robotic female voice said over the loudspeaker.

"Go!" I shouted just as Pearl appeared in front of the window in all her glory.

"Holy shifter," Luka breathed beside me. Bennett

and Talon wasted no time leaping onto Pearl's back, with Marmal's help to steady them, as I bent down to my wolf.

"You have to make sure they don't give Sage another injection. It will be easier to get her out if she's not unconscious. Chew through the binds on her hands and feet and we'll fly down right now and get you both out."

She nodded and then took off, going ghostly as she plowed through the wall.

"Babe!" Sawyer called to me, and I looked up. We were the only two left. He reached out his hand to me. I slipped my cuffs back on and took his outstretched arm.

"Hey, take us with you!" a male snapped behind me. I craned my head to see the rest of the guys who'd been working out when the whole fight began. The one who had spoken was a tall vampire and he was holding a sleek handgun he'd stolen from the guard. His cuffs were still on, which let me know Sawyer hadn't shared the key with them.

'These pricks have been trying to kill me since the day I got here,' Sawyer growled into my head.

I grabbed Sawyer's offered hand. "Sure thing. Let me just check in with my friend," I told him, and stood.

He lifted the gun, and then Sawyer's arms came around my waist, yanking me backward as he jumped. I sailed through the air, landing on top of Sawyer as we both hit Pearl's gigantic back, hard. Marmal and

Sawyer's crew held us in place just as the gun clicked. I steeled myself, ready to catch bullets or whatever magical garbage I would need to, but then nothing happened.

"Needs the guard's fingerprint, you *jerk*," Luka called out.

Sawyer grinned viciously. "Enjoy the next fifty years knowing we got out."

Walsh just flipped the dudes the bird. Then the wind picked up behind us as Pearl started to descend.

Wow, these guys must have had a lot of beef together—stories for another time.

I needed to focus on my bestie.

"Take me to the bottom floor, back side of the building where they are keeping Sage!" I yelled to Marmal.

Everything was happening so fast I couldn't process it properly.

'*I snuck in an elevator, overheard them say they were taking the dead guard down to medical on the first floor,*' my wolf said.

Thank God.

"Sage is here?" Walsh's voice broke.

I looked back at him and noticed the pained expression that crossed his face. I nodded. "She got my wolf inside, but they're holding her on the bottom floor, so we need to get her."

As Pearl flew down the eighty floors to the bottom, I watched the flickering lights inside. Red and white flashes pulsed as the siren wailed and the robot voice played out over a loudspeaker: "Prison break. Lockdown procedures active. Shield down. Remain in your cells."

My wolf pulled my attention and I focused on her just in time to see her enter Sage's room. She was still lying motionless in the bed with cloth straps around her feet and arms. The cloth bands were connected with silver chains, but my wolf had already started to chew at the band on her right arm, sawing it with her back teeth.

Sage moaned.

'*Sage, wake up!*' I used our pack bond to rouse her. '*I got the guys. Walsh and Sawyer are safe. We need to get you out of there.*'

I felt her consciousness stir. '*Demi?*' she rasped through our bond.

My wolf looked up at her just as she opened her eyes and the cuff fell away from her right hand. She slowly brought her hand up to pet my wolf's head, and then nodded as if coming out of a deep sleep.

'*I'm so groggy,*' she said.

'*It's okay. Just try to help undo your binds. I'm almost to you.*'

Sage lazily reached over and started to unclip the left arm binding as my wolf chewed on the left leg loop. Once she got her hands free, she sat up, looking more alert, and helped get out of the binds at her feet just as voices could be heard shouting down the hallway.

'*Open the blinds of the window behind you. I can't tell which one is yours,*' I instructed her as Pearl flew low to the ground between the building and the thirty-foot-high security wall. We were trapped here if they got the protection back up. We needed out of here.

Stat.

The blinds of the window to my left ripped open then and Sage and my wolf peered at us from inside. Relief exploded in my chest at the sight of my bestie.

'Now back away from the window! We're going to smash it open!' I told her. She moved back and Sawyer looked at me with fascination as he sat behind me, hands gripped tightly on my hips.

"Are you communicating with her?" he asked suddenly as she and my wolf backed away from the window.

"They're pack," was all I said, and then I gave Marmal a curt nod. When I looked back at Sawyer, his face was frozen in shock. Mouth open, eyes wide, I knew the fact that I'd made Sage my pack would hit him hard. She was his cousin after all.

Pack. He mouthed the word in confusion. Sage was his, Marmal was a troll, but I didn't have time for this conversation right now.

Pearl set herself onto the ground and then retracted her wings so that she could inch closer to the window on foot. Her tail flicked once and then everyone on her back flinched as the window shattered. Talon and Walsh sat side by side, legs tucked under them as they gripped horns like handles. Luka and Bennett did the same behind them. There wasn't much more room, especially for a long flight home, but we'd make it work.

Back in the room with my wolf, she and Sage huddled together as the shattered glass blew out everywhere. Shards littered the linoleum floor as Sage charged forward to escape. I didn't need to tell her that time was of the essence. She felt it.

On Pearl, Walsh shifted away from us, and his booted foot extended onto the windowsill to brace himself as he reached out a hand for Sage. My attention snapped back to my body, making sure that with Walsh's shifting weight, I wasn't going to be thrown off of the giant dragon we all somehow teetered on. Sage leapt onto the windowsill, and then Walsh gripped her by the waist and pulled her into him. She embraced him fully, wrapping her arms and legs around him as his hands came up to wind in her hair and I smiled.

We did it.

Looking over at my wolf who stood deep inside of the room, I patted my chest. "Come on! Jump!"

Why was she so far back?

Oh, the glass! It was everywhere and would tear up her paws. I could sense her figuring out what to do when the door behind her burst off its hinges and then red-hot pain sliced through my wolf's rib cage. The mother of all electric shocks rocked her body and she fell to the ground shaking as I stood on top of Pearl and screamed.

"NO!"

There, standing just behind my incapacitated wolf, was the vile vampire queen. She held some kind of Taser device, and when she turned a dial, my body and wolf simultaneously felt like it was consumed by fire. Every nerve ending frayed and the world spun and sweat broke out on my body. My wolf shook, her teeth chattering as the electricity rocked her small form. My human self lunged forward, placing one foot on the windowsill, and was reaching over with my left arm to remove my right cuff when one of the tall fey guards from the gym room, who was clearly no longer unconscious, burst into the room, gun raised.

It all happened so fast, too fast. The muzzle of the gun flickered with light and then something sharp pinched my stomach. Fresh, hot warmth trickled down into my underwear, and I swayed. I flew backward into someone's arms and then Sawyer screamed. It was gut-wrenching and inhumane as it turned into a howl.

It took a moment for me to realize he was screaming for me.

"No! You idiot! I need her alive." The queen's voice sounded warbled and my body shook. "Cuff the wolf and bring up the protection field," the queen snapped.

Then Sawyer said the three most horrible words I'd ever heard. "Go! Leave her!"

Without even considering another option, Pearl kicked off the ground and her wings snapped out as she pumped us high into the air. My wolf lay on the ground inside of the room shaking and whimpering from the high-voltage electric current pulsing nonstop into her body.

Everything felt so light and cold... I was *so* cold. My teeth chattered as we flew further and further away from my wolf, the other half of my soul, my savior.

"Sawyer don't...make me... I can't," I rasped. There was pressure on my stomach, and I looked down to see a panicked and wide-eyed Walsh trying to plug all of the holes there.

Oh my God. There were so many holes in my body. How was I still conscious?

In that moment, the shock wore off and the woozy heaviness of sleep pressed down on me along with a pain so horrifying I nearly passed out.

This was how I died. I knew it. Felt it deep inside of my soul.

I reached up with bloody fingers and trailed them down Sawyer's cheek. "I want you to know..." I rasped, as breathing became too hard. "That you were loved. Not for your money, or because of some stupid mating year. I..." Why was breathing so hard? Sawyer's eyes filled with tears as he shook his head in complete denial of the situation. "I loved you so madly and wildly. I want you to...know...that. Tell Creek that...I loved him too. Unlike any other." Once the last word slipped from my lips, a deep, heavy blackness, unlike any I'd ever felt before, washed over me and pulled me under, like a tsunami dragging a victim to their grave.

CHAPTER EIGHT

SAWYER

S HE WENT LIMP IN MY ARMS AND EVERY RATIONAL thought left me. This wasn't happening. Not like this. "Demi!" I shook her lightly, but her head just lolled onto my lap.

No, no, no. Hell no. Not her, not the love of my life...

"Take off the cuffs!" Sage half sobbed as those of us who knew her best lost our collective minds. Walsh ripped her cuffs off and I once again cursed myself for making them. These things hurt her more times than they helped her.

"With the cuffs off, will she heal?" I asked my best friend. My voice sounded hollow, and even I knew that there was no healing from this, not without a trauma team and top-notch hospital, which we didn't have anymore. It had been bombed by the damn vampires.

My heart thundered in my chest as I gripped my dying wife's blood-soaked T-shirt.

Think. Breathe. Hell.

"Astra." Walsh's voice was barely a whisper. We were flying on a dragon over the entire city of Light Fey and no one looked at us, which made me think the dragon had some type of cloaking ability.

"What?" I couldn't concentrate. All of my medical schooling was trying to take up residence in my brain at the same time as my grief and it was short-circuiting my brain. Demi wasn't someone I could fathom living without. I tried in prison and almost committed suicide. I'd never loved a creature so much as I adored and worshiped this woman in my arms. She couldn't die. Not like this. Not after everything we'd been through.

"Astra! Is that chick still alive?" Walsh screamed at Sage.

Sage's face brightened, which gave me hope as I remembered the story of the Paladin priestess healing Walsh when he was injured...near death.

I looked up at the troll girl who seemed to be in charge of the dragon. "Take us to Astra."

She looked confused. *Damn.* Why did she look confused?

"Paladin Village, in the Wild Lands, I'll show you the way," Sage barked. The troll nodded and her named popped into my mind. *Marmal.* This must be Marmal from Demi's time stuck in the Magic Lands.

There was so much blood. Even with Walsh and I plugging holes, they bled through to her back. My gaze flicked up to Luka, whose eyes were practically glowing with hunger. Her blood, it would be nearly impossible to resist for him, especially since they half-starved him in prison. "You good, bro?" I asked.

He swallowed hard and nodded, looking away from Demi. I trusted him with my life, we knew everything about each other, the last year had brought us closer than brothers. If he felt himself losing control, he'd jump off this dragon before harming my wife. He knew what she meant to me.

If I had a surgical kit and operating room, I might be able to do something. Right now I was utterly useless... about to put all of my faith in a teenage girl with supposed healing powers...

My mind calculated any other option. We could fly into downtown Light Fey City and take Demi to their hospital, but odds are they wouldn't treat her once they found out she was responsible for the prison break. We were already over Dark Fey Territory, coming up on Troll Village. There was no turning back now.

My fingers plugged holes inside of the tiny stomach that once held my son I'd never met. I had an out-of-body experience then. How was this real? Everything was going fine. Demi was in my arms. We'd almost had her wolf. How was this happening?

Walsh ripped his shirt into strips as he tried in vain

to stop the bleeding. How could someone so small bleed so much?

God, please don't take her. I reached out to the universe. I was a man of science, not one of spirituality, but I could be persuaded to believe in anything right now.

Anything for Demi.

Reaching up with my free hand, I did something I'd been scared to do since she lost consciousness. I felt for a pulse at her neck.

'Hold on, my love.' I tried to find her through our bond, like maybe there I could save her, hold her somehow...but she was all dark, gone. It left me feeling empty, and the desperation I'd initially felt when I first landed in prison fell over me like a thick fog.

Thumps lightly beat against my finger. *Thump. Thump.* I froze. It was faint, but she had a pulse.

"Please go faster!" I growled at the female troll. She peered back at Demi limp in my arms and soaked in blood and all the color drained from her face. Tears lined her eyes, rolling down her cheeks, and she nodded.

I had yet to meet a person who truly knew Demi and didn't absolutely love her. Even the troll woman did, you could see it in her eyes. If Demi died, the devastation that it would leave behind would be felt by every single person who knew her.

I can't think like that right now.

Sage was fumbling with a cell phone. Why, I didn't know. There was no one to call. We had no hospital and I was assuming the medical ward in Paladin Village wasn't equipped for this.

"Eugene, Demi's been shot. Tell Astra to prepare to heal her," Sage said quickly into the phone, and a flicker of hope surged inside of me.

If Astra really could heal someone near death, if she was waiting and ready when we landed...maybe Demi would make it...

As we flew over the tall gothic buildings of Vampire City, my face turned into a scowl. The vampires were responsible for nearly every recent problem in my life. Looking back, I glanced at Luka, the only decent blood-sucker I knew. He wore a mask of pain; it danced across his face before slipping away into a cold hard stare. After what Luka had been through, what it must be like right now to look down on his old home...I couldn't imagine it. He met my gaze and I nodded once.

He returned it.

That was that. An unspoken bond. I would take his story to the grave with me, but he knew I knew, and that meant he wasn't alone. Sometimes grief needed to be shared or it would suffocate you under the weight of it. Luka had shared his grief with me, and now I carried a little bit of it so that he could breathe. Hypothetically, since vampires didn't actually breathe.

Demi's pulse fluttered under my index finger and I whimpered, my focus back on her. She had to make it, she just had to.

The dragon started to descend over the Wild Lands as Sage barked directions from her place behind me. I'd never been to Paladin Village. I'd grown up hating their people, and when I'd finally wanted to go there, to be with Demi and support her, I'd had that damn ankle monitor on.

"Come on!" I shouted, knowing that yelling wouldn't help anything, but it made me feel slightly better anyway.

If the medical ward there had an IV kit, I could at the very least transfer some of my blood to Demi. My mind raced with medical knowledge and procedures I could try if only I had the right tools. Next year I would have started medical school, but I did enough in my training that I knew how to suture and do an intravenous vein puncture.

I wondered if Dr. Pearson had survived the past year and if he was in the village right now. He was the top surgeon we had, but without the right tools or a proper operating room...

"There!" Sage pointed to a thicket of trees, and I looked just past them at what I assumed was Paladin Village.

Pearl descended and I gleaned a closer look.

Whoa. Shock ripped through me as my gaze fell on the wooden fence, tips sharpened to points. Inside was not the rough and tumble encampment I assumed it would be. I mean, it clearly had taken a beating, with some buildings looking like they were shelled out by bombs, but most of them were intact, and made fully of brick. Thousands of tents and makeshift huts dotted the roadways and open areas, and my heart swelled with hope that some of those people were my pack.

I looked down at Demi.

Our pack.

There was no them or us anymore. It was *we.* Paladin, city wolf, we needed to unite if we wanted to end this war, and that started right here with Demi and I. Together. I looked back up at the farmlands in the distance and was surprised to see the rolling green hills dotted with row upon row of food. It looked like corn and lettuce and other edible things. I realized then that the Paladins had something that the city wolves didn't: a knowledge they could teach us so that we might just survive the next few months.

The dragon tried to find a spot to land, but there were people everywhere. Children running and playing. Tents and backpacks littered the roads.

Demi's heartbeat suddenly stopped and panic surged so quickly inside of me that my wolf nearly lurched out of my body.

"She's crashing!" I shouted, as alpha power slapped out of me and pressed in on everyone riding the dragon.

Sage pointed to an open spot where the small girl with mousy brown hair waved us over. I remembered her from the one time we met, but somehow she looked even smaller now, younger too. She wore some kind of feathered headdress and bone-carved necklace, but she looked like a kid trying to play chief.

This was her? *The great healer?*

My head snapped to Walsh: "The second we hit the ground, I need you to find Dr. Pearson…if he's still alive. If not, any of the city wolf surgeons will do."

Walsh nodded, and then the dragon's talons hit the earth.

It was like time had stopped or slowed down; the next few moments felt so long. I felt out of my body trying to understand what to do and how I could help Demi. Luka assisted me in carrying her to the ground, but that just made Demi lose more blood, and I wasn't even sure she was still alive at this point.

No pulse…why can't I feel a pulse?

So much blood.

Astra, all of maybe seventeen, walked over to Demi and her eyes flashed a glowing blue.

"Heal her please. I beg of you." I looked up at the girl, my fingers still plugging holes in my lifeless wife as tears lined my eyes, and I nearly lost my damn mind in front of all these people. My heart felt like it was going to explode in my chest, like someone had reached in and squeezed it so hard it might pop like a balloon at any moment.

Astra looked over at me with such strength and confidence then, I wondered if I had underestimated her.

With a simple nod, she fell to her knees and clasped her hands in prayer.

"Father, we need a miracle. Use me, make me your vessel of light and healing." The girl raised her clasped hands to the sky.

Demi said that the Paladins were super spiritual, but I hadn't experienced it firsthand. I didn't mind. I wasn't here to judge, and if it saved my wife, I would pray to the Father every night for the rest of my life.

A scream rang out from behind me, raising the hairs on my arms and I spun. Demi's mom stood directly behind me, face stricken as she stared down at her unconscious daughter. A small baby boy with dark hair and blue eyes was in her arms, and my heart shattered. I swallowed down a sob as I reached for my son with my free hand. A crowd of people had started to gather around, and Eugene was pushing them back, but I didn't care about any of that. Nothing mattered to me in that moment except holding this beautiful boy that Demi and I made. Demi's mom reached out and deposited Creek in my arms before she fell into a puddle of tears, her husband pulling her into a tight hug.

Her grief killed me, but all my pain washed away the moment I looked down at my son. His round, wide eyes looked up at me with an innocence that I clung to and hoped he would always have. Knowing that Demi carried him and birthed him all on her own out in the wild, it made me love and respect her ten times more than I had before she left for her alpha trial. Demi was the strongest woman I knew. I'd seen the fire and strength of an alpha that first day I'd met her at Delphi. To be honest, it scared me sometimes, because I wasn't sure in what world two alphas could co-exist, but now I knew. *This world.* If anyone could come back from death, it was her. We would remake the world together with our son. Born of both cultures. A symbol of our love and unification. I could smell his wolf inside of him, still young but strong, and I was grateful for that.

Holding his tiny body to my chest, I turned back around just in time to see a blue mist fall from the sky, coating Astra like a magical rain.

The crowd gasped in awe, but all I could do was hope. Hope that this young girl was powerful enough to save the love of my life.

Reaching out, I grabbed Demi's cold, limp hand, and tucked Creek up against my chest between his mother and me.

"He needs you. I need you," I begged her, as if she had a choice, as if my words could somehow bring her back from wherever her spirit had wandered. The blue sparkle raining down on Astra became so bright then that I had to close my eyes and shield Creek's face with my chest.

As I held my wife's hand, our newborn son cradled between us, I prayed to every god imaginable that she would heal and wake up so that we could be a family again, because no woman compared to her.

"Get back!" Astra shouted, but her voice was not her

own. It was deep, barely human, and *full* of power. The force of that power slapped against me, as if trying to push me back. I jerked Creek away, yanking my fingers out of Demi's abdomen, and rolled onto my side just as the blue mist exploded out of Astra's body. It rose up slightly into the air and then shot down into Demi with the force of a million tiny bullets.

Holy shifter.

Demi's body seized and jerked wildly as the blue light pelted into her like hail dropping from the sky. Astra arched her back, letting loose with a wail of pain and I frowned. Was this normal? I should have asked more about the healing with Walsh. I should have asked more about the Paladins. I'd been so dismissive of them, and Demi never talked about them, probably for fear of upsetting me. I was going to do better after this, take an interest in her people.

Our people.

I would care for them as if they were my own, as she had clearly done for the city wolves in my absence.

Astra's wail grew in intensity and I backed up, getting to my feet and handing Creek off to Sage.

Something wasn't right. This didn't feel normal. Why was the healer in pain?

"Are you okay?" I asked Astra, looking from her to Demi with a frown.

Demi had stopped convulsing, and I shook my head in disbelief when my gaze narrowed to her shredded and bleeding stomach—or what *had* been her torn open and bleeding stomach. Now it was…healed. Five metal shell casings littered the floor underneath her rib cage as if they'd been magically pushed out.

What the hell kind of healer was this girl?

I looked up in absolute joy to thank her, then I noticed blood blooming in Astra's abdomen. That's when she started to fall.

Moving quickly, I rushed forward, leaping over Demi to catch Astra. She collapsed into my arms as the crowd broke into sobs. I gathered from the headdress and amazing healing abilities that she was important to these people, and now I was at a loss of what to do.

I knew she was their priestess, but I didn't know culturally what that equated to. President? Pastor? Mother Teresa?

"Get a doctor!" I shouted, moving Astra to her back so that I could start plugging holes in her stomach just as I'd done for Demi. She had bullet holes in the same place that Demi had.

What the hell kind of sorcery is this?

Chills ran up my arms when I realized what Astra had done. She'd *taken* Demi's injury, not healed it. She took it into herself. A small, innocent seventeen-year-old girl.

"Dammit. I'm so sorry. I didn't know," I told the girl, reliving the nightmare I'd just went through with Demi, but now with a stranger that I somehow felt responsible for.

Astra reached up, grabbing the sides of my face, and smiled sweetly. "Take care of Demi. She's special." Her voice was weak, too weak.

No.

I looked over at Demi just in time to see her chest rise with a giant breath as she gulped in lungfuls of air.

Oh, thank God! She was alive, and I'd killed her most cherished pack member.

She is going to kill me.

CHAPTER NINE

W HAT DID YOU DO!?" MY VOICE CROAKED AS I gasped for air and rolled onto my side to see Sawyer holding a bleeding Astra in his arms. I remembered getting pumped full of bullets and then losing consciousness on Pearl. Now Sawyer held Astra, who was bleeding from the stomach in the exact places that I had.

She'd healed me.

No!

Dizziness and panic slammed into me as I tried to remember what had happened when she'd healed Walsh. How had I helped her? I'd claimed her...but now she was already mine.

Mine.

My alpha power surged inside of me and I sat up, reaching out to take her from Sawyer, who looked crestfallen at the seemingly dead teenager in his lap.

There was so much blood...

Sawyer released her and I pulled her to my chest, tears brimming in my eyes. There weren't many people that I truly cared about like I cared for this girl. Her faith in me, her belief that I would return from the Wild Lands and save the Paladin people, kept me alive in my darkest moments in the woods.

'Astra...take from me what you need. You're mine. You have to stay with me. I need you.' I spoke into her mind, latching on to her soul with my alpha power. I felt my power, like small tendrils, hooking into Astra's energy and pulling her back from wherever she was drifting off to.

'Careful, Alpha. You could kill the both of you.' Rab's warning washed ice-cold fear down my veins and I froze.

Willow knelt beside me, fanning sage smoke at the both of us. "You can't take too much of the injury from her. She'll need to be the one to heal that wound. Just take enough to keep her alive. Otherwise, you'll take it all back into yourself and you'll both perish." Willow's voice shook. I nodded, and the realization that I was about to do some very serious and advanced magic with zero training came over me.

"Demi..." Sawyer's voice pulled my attention and I snapped my head up to look at him.

'Don't you dare tell me not to save this sweet girl,' I growled through our bond, and he balked, looking guilty, before nodding and lowering his head in submission.

Taking in a deep breath, I let my intuition guide me. My power was so enmeshed with Astra's soul, it was hard to tell where she began and I ended. My stomach cramped as I pushed energy into her and she sucked it from me like a vacuum. I could feel the magic leaving me in gushes and I gasped as more pain sliced into my stomach.

"That's enough!" Sawyer yelled, stepping forward, but Rab was quick and positioned himself between Sawyer and I.

"She's got this," Rab stated, staring down my husband.

I couldn't focus my attention on the dominant male pissing match, I had to concentrate on this energy and power that I felt. I needed Astra to regain consciousness before I pulled my magic back.

'Astra...come back,' I whimpered, the pain in my stomach growing unbearable.

Just when I thought that I would die from this agony, it eased, and Astra's eyes snapped open.

"Alpha." She looked at me weakly and I felt the power she'd sucked from me so freely shut off like a faucet.

The pain stopped and I reached for her shirt, pulling it up to see there were puckered holes there. They looked red and angry, some still bleeding, but closing slowly.

Relief rushed through me. I wanted to shake her for doing such a stupid thing as risking herself for me, but thought better of it.

"Don't do that again. Don't die for me. *Ever*," I told her angrily. I loved this girl. Somehow along the way she'd become like a little sister to me.

She gave me a small smile, a smile that said she would do it all over again, and I just shook my head in disbelief.

Walsh showed up just then with the only remaining pack surgeon we had left at his side.

"Get her into medical and make sure she's not internally bleeding," I snapped to Dr. Pearson. "I think it's sealed but...she needs fluids, and let me know if we need to donate blood."

He nodded, bending down with Walsh to take her.

Willow placed a hand on mine. "I'll go with her. Make sure she's okay."

I squeezed her hand. "Thank you."

Everyone had gathered in rows and rows of people, fanning outward into the village, to see the big show. Their eyes went from me, covered in blood, to Sawyer, their alpha fresh out of prison, and then to Luka, a traitorous vampire on our lands, before finally resting on Pearl, the damn dragon that no one knew existed until now.

'*Please make them leave. I can't right now. I need to process,*' I told Sawyer, looking down at my bloody clothes.

I...died. I remembered this bright light, and then I was floating among the stars looking down on the planet

149

from thousands of miles away. I remembered Sawyer's voice calling me home, and then Astra's energy, before being sucked back violently.

Now I wanted time with my baby and more time with Sawyer. I needed to regroup and I didn't want my people to see me weak like this.

"These men..." Sawyer pointed to Luka, Bennett, and Talon. "...are here as my guests. They will *not* be harmed." His voice was clear. That was an order and a threat. "Get back to your tents and continue your chores. We'll have a pack meeting tomorrow to discuss our plan to get Wolf City back."

There was a chorus of cheers at that and everyone disbanded. When the meadow was clear of most of the people, Sawyer reached down and pulled me into his arms, lifting me up off the ground. "Are you hurt?" His voice was gruff.

I shook my head. "Creek?" I looked around and Sawyer nodded, walking me over to Sage.

Sage handed me my son and I pulled him into my chest, a sob ripping from my throat. I missed him so much. Babies, puppies, and new cars all had this distinct smell, and Creek was no different. I wanted to bottle it and keep it forever; he smelled so fresh and clean.

He leaned into me, trying to nurse through my shirt, causing Sawyer to chuckle. "Looks like I've got competition."

I grinned. "Take us home. I want one night as a family. Tomorrow we can plan a war."

He nodded, and I told Rab to make our guests comfortable giving them whatever they needed, including Pearl. Then Sage led the way to our small but quaint two-bedroom cottage across from Astra's meeting hall-church. The second Sawyer stepped inside, I could see that he was impressed. His approving gaze ran over the handcrafted furniture and then into the kitchen.

"You can set me down." I held on to Creek, who was now asleep.

Sawyer shook his head. "Where's the bedroom?"

Sage pointed down a hall and he nodded, walking in quick strides through the living room and kitchen and down the hallway into my room.

"Astra gave me this place, got it all ready for me," I told him. Everything that was adorable and handmade in this home was because of Astra. I wanted him to know that.

He nodded, looking around with a reverence. "It's nice. She's a very special girl and I'm grateful to her."

She'd better be okay. I could never live with myself if she wasn't. I felt so empty and depressed knowing she was sick right now, healing from injuries I had sustained. I didn't feel like myself, I felt empty, sad, and...off. I was about to say as much when the truth of what I'd just said knocked into me like a truck. In all the drama of almost dying, I'd totally forgotten.

My wolf.

'I'm so sorry!' I sobbed as I reached out to her through our bond, horrified that I'd forgotten her for a moment in all the near-death drama. But she didn't answer. She was cuffed, gagged, cut off from me as I was from Sawyer when I'd been in a similar situation.

Sawyer looked down at me, seemingly confused at my sudden sobfest.

"Sawyer, my wolf," I croaked, the full weight and emptiness of knowing half of my soul was in prison while I was free settling into me.

He nodded solemnly, setting Creek and I on the bed as he crawled in beside us. "I know. I'm so sorry, my love."

"But..." My eyes brimmed over with tears and Sawyer reached up and cupped my chin, forcing me to look at him.

I was met with the fiery yellow gaze of his wolf.

"Demi Calloway-Hudson, I will *not* let anything bad happen to any part of you. I promise." His voice was barely human, thick with his wolf, and I nodded, trusting in him.

I needed to lean on him right now, because where I was, it was too dark, and he was my beacon of light.

Lying together with our son between us, I couldn't help but think that my wolf had again sacrificed something so that I could be free.

'I'm sorry,' I told her. *'I'm so sorry.'*

I rested my forehead on Sawyer's, and we both lay there a long time before I finally got up and showered off all the dried blood. Then we fell asleep, for the first time as a family.

———•—•———

Creek cried for a bottle in the middle of the night and I groggily got up to make one. Shuffling with my baby out into the kitchen, I found that Sage already had one in her hands. "Heard him crying. I'll take him until morning." She tipped her head at the room Sawyer slept in and gestured for me to go back and lay with him.

I was so exhausted after nearly dying, I wasn't going to argue. I nodded gratefully and shuffled back down the hallway. Slipping in bed beside Sawyer, I tried not to wake him, but he stirred anyway.

"Is it the baby? Need help?" he asked, rubbing his eyes and sitting up. "I'm up. I'll change a diaper or whatever you need."

Bleary-eyed, he looked at me through tousled hair and long lashes. Shirtless, covered in tattoos, Sawyer had never looked sexier. This new felon Sawyer was hot as all hell, and my body suddenly thrummed to life with need.

"Sage has him." I inched closer to him and he froze.

It had been a year since either of us had touched each

other, and our bodies seemed to realize it at this very moment.

Reaching out, he grabbed my hips and pulled me closer to him as I clung to his neck, bringing his face closer to mine.

Our mouths met in a hungry, messy, sexy-as-all-hell kiss. It burned with fire and passion the likes of which I'd never seen from him before. We were hungry for each other in a way that felt almost dangerous, in a way that almost hurt. I raked my nails along his neck, down to his abs, not caring if I pushed a little too hard. I wanted to claim him, I wanted to *devour* him.

He was *mine*.

A growl ripped from his throat and then suddenly he was on top of me, pinning me underneath him.

I'd dreamed about this for so long at the cabin in the woods. Being with Sawyer again, making love.

"God, I missed you," Sawyer huffed.

I looked up at him, noticing that this Sawyer was new. He was so strong and sure of himself. And it was completely and utterly the sexiest thing alive. I looked up into his chiseled chest and stared at the word *Demi* tattooed over his heart.

Reaching down, he threaded his fingers into the back of my hair, and his eyes flashed yellow as our imprint seemed to come alive. It was like it was a living thing, trying to show the other person how much we cared for one another. I was everything to Sawyer, I *felt* that.

He adored me, he possessively wanted to provide for and protect me and Creek, and he would let the whole world burn before allowing one more bad thing to happen to me.

Now that I had Sawyer back, I knew there was nothing we couldn't do so long as we were together.

CHAPTER TEN

THE NEXT MORNING, SAWYER AND I SHOWERED together and then stepped out into the living room, where Sage was asleep with Creek on the couch. Her back was facing the open room and Creek was tucked between her and the couch back so he wouldn't fall off. She had the best motherly instincts. I was so grateful to have her help in raising him.

Reaching over, I shook her shoulder gently. "Go get some rest," I told her, "I'll take over now."

She looked bleary-eyed from me to Creek, and then nodded, planting a kiss on Creek's forehead. She shuffled off to her bedroom.

Sawyer swooped in beside me and replaced the empty spot where Sage had just been, raising his arm above his head so that he could lie on it and stare down at our son. "You and Sage did all of this alone? In the woods with no diapers or anything?"

I could feel the pain in his voice, regret and shame. I knew he wanted to be there for me and Creek, I felt it through our bond.

"Yep. We made do," I told him.

Sawyer nodded. "You're amazing. Tell me everything. I want to help take care of him. How often do we feed him, when should I change his diaper, *how* do I change his diaper?"

Creek stirred at the sound of Sawyer's voice and I giggled. "Well, first off," I whispered. "When a baby is sleeping, try not to use your loud alpha voice right in his ear."

Sawyer looked up at me, terrified. "Oh. Damn," he whispered, just as Creek started to cry.

"And we feed him now. Take your finger and stick it near his mouth. If he starts sucking on it, he's hungry."

Sawyer's eyes widened. Taking the finger of his free hand, he put it near Creek's mouth and Creek started to suckle on it, calming his cries instantly.

"Whoa," Sawyer said, and I laughed again, running into the kitchen to mix some formula.

Over the next hour, I gave Sawyer a Baby 101 class. I taught him how to feed and burp Creek, how to change a diaper, and the different ways to carry him, which was easier now that his neck wasn't floppy and he could hold his head up.

"I love him," Sawyer mused, as Creek reached up and played with the scruff of his beard. "I've only known about him for a week, and met him for half a day, and I utterly and truly would die for him."

I beamed, raking my fingers through Sawyer's hair. "Welcome to parenting."

Sawyer looked over at me with one of those panty-dropping smiles, the ones he used to give me at Sterling Hill, but then his face fell. "You must have been so scared, so alone out there. I—I can't imagine it, Demi."

I nodded. "I was. But those woods made me into the strong woman I am today. Without them, I'm not sure I would have what it takes to do what we will need to in order to defeat the vampires."

Sawyer inclined his head. "You have ideas?"

I did. "You?"

"Yep," Sawyer said. "I think it's time we called a meeting and made a plan. Every day those vampires sit there and get more comfortable in our city, they increase their hold on our land."

My heart flipped over in my chest. "Our land?"

The Paladin lands were mine. City was his. Did he expect me to go there and live with him full time after we expelled the vampires? To leave the Paladin people behind? He seemed to guess my thinking and shook his head.

"Our land. Our pack. Paladin and city, as one." His voice was thick with emotion, and I knew it was one of the hardest things he'd probably ever said in his life. This pack, my pack, cursed his family for years, causing them to take wives for all the wrong reasons. Forgetting all that, starting fresh, it was a big deal, one I did not take lightly.

I gestured around the small cottage. "I know it's not a fancy glass mansion with solar panels and a Range Rover in the garage, but I was thinking when we get Wolf City back, we could spend half the time here."

Sawyer grinned. "Honey, I just spent the last year in prison with a vampire prince as a roommate. This is amazing."

My skin prickled at the words "vampire prince." "Luka?"

Sawyer's brow furrowed, and he seemed like he was cursing himself for telling me.

"Luka is a prince?" My mind reeled at that. "That means...he's the queen's son! He's Vicon's brother?" My jaw dropped open as shock slammed into me. How could Sawyer become best friends with the brother of the man who *raped* me, the entire reason he went to jail!

Sawyer's eyes widened in horror. "No. He's the queen's nephew. *She* jailed him so that he couldn't take over the monarchy. He hates her."

I relaxed a little, but only just a little. Luka was a Drake! He shared DNA with the evilest woman alive.

Sawyer stood, set Creek down on his little handmade play mat, and faced me. "Demi, when Walsh and I first arrived, every inmate on the eightieth floor had it out for us. It was only later we found out that the queen had said that anyone who killed us in prison would be released from their sentence early, no questions asked."

I gasped. That was a low blow.

He nodded. "We were ganged up on daily, beaten within an inch of our lives. The only reason I'm alive today is because Luka jumped in one day and fought back with us. Then the next day Bennett, and the next day Talon."

Tears filled my eyes at that, and my gaze fell to the tattoo on his collarbone. "Five Crew."

He nodded. "Once there were five of us, people realized it wasn't worth it. They backed off or they got broken bones," he growled.

Holy smokes, I'd had no idea what he'd been through. It was time to put away my prejudice and accept Sawyer's new friends as family. Even if one of them was a rotten Drake.

"They're welcome here as long as they like," I managed to croak out.

Reaching up, Sawyer cupped my face in his hands. "I know this past year apart has been hard, but I think it's only made us stronger."

I smiled, leaning forward to capture his mouth in a kiss.

When he pulled back, he took my hands in his and looked down at them. "Where's your wedding ring?"

I winced. "I gave it to Seam for insider knowledge on how to break you out of prison. Sorry…"

Sawyer grinned. "I mean, if you had to trade your wedding ring, that's a pretty good excuse."

"Yeah, I had to bail my felon out of jail." I lightly punched his arm.

Sawyer chuckled, a full belly chuckle, and it warmed my heart. We were together, out of the Dark Woods, out of prison, and with our son. It was almost perfect.

Almost.

"They'll be looking for you," I told Sawyer. By now the jailbreak was all over the supernatural news. It was only a matter of time before they started looking here.

Sawyer sighed. "And you."

Wasn't that depressing? The two leaders, the people our pack needed the most, and we were the biggest danger to them.

There was a knock at the door and Sawyer crossed the room to open it. Luka, Bennett, and Talon stood there, and Sawyer invited them inside. Creek had fallen asleep, passed out on his little rabbit fur play mat that Sage had made him.

Luka's eyes were nearly black, and there were dark circles under them. A vampire's natural sleep time was just about now, as the morning sun was coming up. They could go out in the sunlight but didn't do well. It looked like Luka wasn't feeling so hot.

"What's up?" Sawyer's voice held concern as he looked over his friend.

Luka reached behind his neck and scratched it, a

sliver of his tan abdomen peeking out of his black T-shirt. "I need to feed. Missed last night and this morning."

Oh.

Ohhh.

Sawyer was less shocked than I, probably because he'd been living with the dude for a year.

"You can feed from me if you need to, and I can put out a call for volunteers to keep you supplied in the future." Sawyer's voice was calm, like he hadn't just offered to let a vampire *feed* from him. Something surged inside of me, some need to protect him.

Alpha Sawyer letting a male vampire *feed* from him. It was...mind blowing.

'He's done it a couple times before,' Sawyer spoke into my mind. He must have felt my anxiety. *'They tried to starve him and kill him in prison. I kept him alive. I don't like it, but I'd do anything for him. He's one of my best friends, Demi.'* Sawyer had to keep drilling that in my head, because clearly it was hard for me to understand. Damn, it was so hard to just be thrown into each other's lives like this. Not knowing or remembering who the new person was.

'Okay,' I told him, trying to be supportive.

"Actually..." Luka hesitated. "We were thinking of heading out into the human world, laying low for a while. We will only be a target on your pack if we stay."

I felt the sadness rip through Sawyer in that moment, but he nodded. "All of you?"

The fey and troll nodded as well. "Nothing more here for us, bro," Talon stated. "Nothing but a death sentence. We just said goodbye to Walsh."

They were all wanted felons...that didn't really hit me until now. They couldn't be seen in Magic City without being arrested.

These people were Sawyer's crew, his best friends. The thought of losing them tore at him, but he knew it was necessary. They'd been there for each other to survive, and now it was time to go their own way, do what they needed to do to endure on the outside.

"The hunters will come for you," Sawyer warned.

It was the second time I'd heard of these human hunters...

Luka shrugged. "Hunted here, hunted there, what's the difference? I can handle some weak human hunters."

Bennett laughed, clapping Luka on the back. "Weak is not how I would describe them, brother. My cousin said they're lethal, and not exactly all human."

Luka's eyes went stormy, almost black, as he squinted at Bennett. "Well, my aunt is more lethal, so until the time comes when I can have her killed, I need to hide out somewhere else."

At the mention of killing his aunt, anger surged up inside of me. "She's mine," I growled, stepping forward, and then swallowed when all four guys looked up at me with surprise. I cleared my throat. "I'm sorry, but if anyone is killing your aunt, that honor will be *mine*."

Luka grinned, and holy hell was he hot. He was like a black-haired James Dean.

"All right, well, call me when you do that, Mrs. Alpha, and I'll come home." He tipped his head to me.

Luka then faced Sawyer. "We can stay and fight if you need us. Just say the word. I can be back over here in an hour or two after feeding."

Sawyer waved him off. "Nah, you better go. We don't need anyone else luring the vampires to us." His words might have said go, but the tone of his voice said something else entirely.

Luka looked conflicted as he stared at Sawyer.

"Go on. We'll be fine," Sawyer urged him again.

Luka nodded, handing Sawyer a piece of paper. "This is the number of Bennett's cousin who we'll be staying with."

Sawyer took the paper and tucked it into his pocket. The four guys stood there awkwardly for a moment, until finally Bennett stepped forward and pulled Sawyer into a bro hug, smacking him hard on the back. "I'll never forget that one day at lunch with the tray," he said as they pulled away.

Sawyer and Bennett burst out laughing at the inside joke and I was suddenly overcome with emotion. These dudes had created a bond unlike any other.

Talon was next, hugging Sawyer, before nodding. "Remember, finger to the eye."

Sawyer and the other boys laughed again, and it

made me so damn happy to see that they had these inside jokes, this bond. I also needed to know the details on all these stories later.

Luka was last. He stepped forward slowly and placed one hand on either of Sawyer's shoulders. "I'm glad I didn't kill you when I had the chance," Luka told him with a twinkle of mischief in his eye.

Sawyer grinned. "Oh, please, I'd like to see you try."

Luka chuckled, pulling Sawyer into a quick bro shoulder hug, and smacked him on the back with two flat palms.

"Call me when Demi finds out she has a long-lost sister who looks just like her," Luka stated as he stepped away.

"Screw you." Sawyer ran toward him playfully, fist raised.

Luka beamed, jumping back with vampire speed, just out of Sawyer's reach, and everyone smiled, but then the smiles slipped from their lips one by one.

"Bye, Sawyer," Luka said.

Sawyer cleared his throat. "Yeah, see you later."

"Thanks for getting us out, Demi." Luka bowed his head in respect to me.

I could only nod, seeing their brotherly love had really touched me. I had been wrong to judge Luka as a bad person just because of his family association. It was clear by this display that he was a good man and a good friend to my mate.

As the three guys turned to walk away, I felt Sawyer's sadness rip through my chest. They were his brothers and he wasn't sure when he would see them again. I came up behind him and wrapped my arms around him, resting my head on his back.

"We'll get Wolf City back, kill the queen, and have the biggest, most amazing, delayed wedding reception anyone has ever seen, and we'll invite your friends."

Sawyer spun, taking my face into his big hands, and nodded. "That sounds nice."

I released a huge sigh, the weight of the task ahead stacking on my back like bricks. "But first we need a really good plan."

"Let's get everyone together and figure this out," Sawyer agreed.

CHAPTER ELEVEN

S TAR, RAVEN, EUGENE, RAB, ARROW, SAGE, SAWYER, Walsh, Marmal, and I all stood inside of Astra's church. I'd gone to check on Astra before coming to the meeting and was beyond relieved to find she was healing well from her wounds—my wounds, really. The doctor said it would take a few weeks, but she'd make a full recovery.

Now it was time to take the queen down, before she could harvest my wolf's essence or something bonkers. I had tried to see things from my wolf's point of view, but we were cut off. They'd done some magic to keep her mind closed to me, which was bull crap considering she *was* me! It had to be the cuffs; they locked down our bond like I'd been locked down from communicating with Sawyer. I sensed her fear, but that was all I could get. I just hoped they weren't draining her blood or torturing her.

'I'm going to get you out,' I sent to her, unsure if she could receive it. I had a vague sense of her location, like you would sense where you were upon waking up from sleep, but then it faded like a dream. She was still in Light Fey Territory and I was taking that as a good sign. If the fey allowed the queen to take her to Vampire City, then we would have problems.

"Okay, you all know what we are up against and what needs to happen. The vampires need to be evicted from Wolf City so, who wants to start? We welcome all ideas." Sawyer opened his hands in a gesture of welcome.

Marmal cleared her throat. "I could get at least a hundred trolls to help. We can..." Her cheeks flushed red. "I'm forbidden from speaking of our magic, but we can be of a big help where metal is involved."

Sawyer nodded, and then raised one eyebrow. "Metal like swords and guns? Could you render them obsolete?"

Marmal looked physically uncomfortable and I wondered if she actually couldn't talk about her troll magic, like she was spelled not to.

"She can," I stated, remembering how she'd burst all of the locks from the cages to free Trip's captured animals.

Marmal looked relieved that I had been the one to answer.

"That would be amazing. Yes!" Sawyer said, scribbling something on a piece of paper.

Star raised her hand. "We can protect the trolls while they disarm the vampires of any metal weapons. Create a shield around them."

Sawyer grinned, and I felt his happiness bubble over into me. "Perfect." He wrote it down.

Rab tapped the table. "The queen won't fall for that trap. The second she sees us fighting back collectively, she'll run or hurt Demi's wolf to draw her out."

Silence descended over the table.

He was right. I'd told him just before the meeting that we'd had to leave my wolf behind, and the heartbreaking look he'd given me had almost made me burst into tears.

I nodded. "I have a plan for that."

A wild plan that every single person at this table was going to say no to.

Sawyer must have sensed it was a wild idea, because he turned to me, one eyebrow raised. "Well?" His body was tense, like he was preparing for a fight. The only person who I could make eye contact with while I verbalized this insanity was Sage. She was the only one who would get it.

"I want to use myself as bait to draw the queen into the Dark Woods where I'll have the upper hand and I can kill her." I said it in one big rush and then braced myself for the barrage of comments.

I was not disappointed.

"The place you got lost for A YEAR!" Sawyer yelled.

"Are you bonkers?" Raven shot.

"Alpha, *no*," Rab added.

"You have a son to think about," Eugene reminded me. "What if you get lost for another year?"

"Or the queen kills you out there?" Sawyer said, and chills rushed up my arms. "And we can't get to you, so we never know. I'm *not* okay with that. No way in hell."

Sage hadn't said anything. She just looked at me with compassion, but now held up her hand, cutting Sawyer off when he was about to speak again. "Do you trust that the woods won't deceive you this time?" she asked me.

I nodded. "You saw how they opened, and we made it home. They trust me."

Sage smiled. "They'll help you kill her."

I grinned, mirroring her smile and imagining a giant tree landing on the queen's face. "Exactly."

Sawyer frowned. "What are you guys talking about?"

Sage stood, pulling up her shirt to show a network of scars that ran along her abdomen. Everyone at the table gasped and Walsh let loose a pained whimper.

I'd done my best to protect her during our time there, but most of the wounds Sage had sustained before I found her were permanent, even with werewolf healing.

"I went after Demi, ignoring the advice of the others, and the woods tried to kill me." She pulled her shirt down and placed both palms on the table, leaning toward Sawyer for effect. "They're *alive*. The trees move, the animals don't think for themselves. Everything in that place serves her." She pointed to me. "And attacks everyone else."

Sawyer leaned back in his chair. "Holy crap," he breathed.

Walsh was watching Sage with glowing yellow eyes. I knew they had a lot of unsaid stuff between them and I could see his adoration for her all over his face. But Sage had changed, she wasn't the type to wait around for a guy to man up and declare his feelings for her anymore. Walsh's chance might already be lost, and that made me sad because I knew he loved her and that she loved him back.

Reaching under the table, Sawyer gave my thigh a squeeze, and that one squeeze said so much. It said: *I'm sorry for what you went through*. It said: *I trust you*.

"Okay." His voice was small, as if he'd failed. "You lead the queen into the Dark Woods, but I want to be there too. I won't allow you to go alone."

I shook my head. "Weren't you listening? The trees—"

"I'll bring a damn chainsaw!" Sawyer bellowed to the room. "Demi, I'm not ever going to be separated from you again. *Ever*."

Damn stubborn idiot. "Fine," I growled.

"I'm going too. He will probably get killed without my help." Sage pointed to Sawyer. "And we should bring Creek, because I'm not dealing with some kidnapping situation once the vampires know about my nephew."

She was right. *Damn.* She was *so* right. What if they found out about him…?

"The cabin," I breathed. "Sawyer, Sage, and Creek can wait in the cabin and I'll lure the queen there and kill her."

The thought of seeing the place where I'd birthed my son again filled me with warmth.

"Would the woods hurt Creek?" Sawyer was suddenly rethinking his idea now that it involved our son.

"No," Rab and I said at the same time.

"He's the next Paladin alpha. They will not touch him," Rab added.

The realization of that seemed to dawn on Sawyer and his eyes widened a little. I felt the shock of it through our bond.

'How will our son lead two packs?' Sawyer suddenly asked.

I had no damn clue. *'Problems for future Sawyer and Demi.'*

'Agreed,' Sawyer said, and then looked at the leaders around the table.

"How do we protect the women and children during the fight?" Eugene asked. "We have over a hundred pregnant women."

"What if we got the women, children, and elderly back into the bunker with a week's worth of food while this plays out?" I offered.

Sawyer nodded. "That could work, although I don't expect to be fighting for a week. We need to hit them hard and fast. I want this over in twenty-four hours after we start it."

I blew air through my teeth. "When do we start it?"

Silence descended on the table. No one spoke, no one moved. How did you decide when to start a war that might possibly kill people you cared about?

"Probably sooner rather than later since they're looking for all of you," a familiar voice called from the open doorway.

Luka.

Sawyer stood, grinning. "You missed me, didn't you?"

Luka rolled his eyes. "You know, my aunt can be a real hag, and I thought you might want some help."

Okay, their little bromance was adorable.

Sawyer welcomed Luka to the table.

"Bennett and Talon?"

"In Spokane. I'll meet up with them after I help you."

I had to admit, his loyalty was kinda hot. My eyes flicked to Sage to see if she was drooling over the sexy vampire, but her gaze was pinned on Walsh.

Of course. I then looked at Raven to see her practically undressing Luka with her eyes and I grinned. She must have felt my gaze, because she looked at me and her cheeks pinked. *Hmm, they would make a cute couple.*

"Have you fed?" I asked Luka. He looked better.

Luka tipped his head to me. "Yes, ma'am. I met a nice fey Ithaki in the woods. After she tried to kill me, I had lunch."

Okay...I was no longer attracted to him and was now slightly terrified.

Sawyer was quick to defend his friend. *'He doesn't feed from women without permission. Unless they try to kill him of course.'*

'Of course.'

"Can you compulse?" I asked him point-blank. If he was vampire royalty, the queen's nephew, he had to have some major power.

He stilled, suddenly unmoving more than he was already unmoving. I'd touched a nerve and I wasn't sure why. Maybe it was rude to ask, like the trolls couldn't talk about their magic.

"Because if you can," I tried to explain, "maybe you could help us lure the queen into the Dark Woods."

My compulsion power was still at its baby stage, and I had zero hope that it would work on the queen of the freaking vampires.

He raised one eyebrow. "The Dark Woods?"

I nodded. "They're cursed. I'll have a better chance to fight her there."

"We," Sawyer amended, "will have a better chance to kill the queen there."

"And she wants your blood to siphon your power?" he asked.

I looked at Sawyer, who shrugged. He had clearly told Luka everything.

"Yes," I answered.

"Then you can expect she'll have already fed on your wolf and be fighting fully juiced up." He said it so nonchalantly, like it wasn't the most horrible thing you could *ever* think of.

Fed on my wolf? *Damn.*

My face must have betrayed my shock, because he softened, his strong jaw and predatorial gaze relaxing. "That knowledge will help us to be better prepared. And no one can compulse the queen. She's above all of us in power, linked to all of us in a way that's hard to explain. Similar to your pack bonds, I imagine."

Okay, that was interesting information, and cool of him to share. Maybe this vampire dude wasn't half bad.

"So, you can't help?" My voice was more defeated than I would have liked. I could lure her, like I had before, but I'd be winded by the time I got her to the Dark Woods and I really wanted the element of surprise.

Luka grinned, and it was a feral look of satisfaction, the points of his canines pressing into his bottom lip. "Oh I didn't say that. If there is one thing my aunt wants more than obtaining your power, it's me. She'd like nothing more than to pull my head from my body, but vampire law states you can't kill another royal lest your entire line be slaughtered, and you lose your reigning position."

Wow, he was just giving us all the details on vampire society.

'*Told you he was cool,*' Sawyer said in my mind.

'*Okay fine, you were right,*' I acquiesced.

"So, if she can't kill you, then what makes you think you will make good bait?" Sawyer said what I was thinking.

"She can't kill me. But her lackeys can. They'll get thrown in jail for murder and she won't lose one night's sleep about it. But she'll want to be there to make sure the job is done." He sounded so sure of himself.

"How would the Magical Creature Council even know if it was her or one of her henchmen?" I said. There were so many councils in the supernatural world, but I knew the MCC were involved in sentencing.

Luka looked to Sawyer and something passed between them. They were hiding something...

Sawyer finally nodded, and Luka returned it. "The MCC is made up of one representative from each of the races. The newest witch representative has...a unique power. One that has made court cases and DNA testing obsolete."

The table started to murmur at that. What kind of power could make an entire court hearing and presenting evidence no longer necessary?

"She's a human lie detector," Star said so suddenly I jumped. I'd forgotten she was here. "She can invade your memories, displaying them on a blank wall like a movie projector."

Hot. Damn. What?

"What do you mean? She can replay Luka's death to

see who really killed him and free the queen of guilt?" I asked.

Star nodded, but Luka held up a hand. "For the record, I don't plan on dying."

"Right," I muttered, completely frazzled by this latest development.

It hit me then why Luka and Sawyer shared that look. Why Sawyer's case and sentencing had been moved up so quickly.

"Sawyer, did she...?" My voice cracked.

His hand slipped under the desk and squeezed my thigh. *'It's okay,'* he said, and everyone looked down at their hands as if inspecting their nails.

'She saw you kill Vicon, but I wasn't there to show what he did to me, to testify on your behalf, so they sentenced you to death.' Tears filled my eyes and a deep sense of regret washed over me. *'Sawyer, I'm so sorry.'* Sawyer spent a year in prison because I'd chosen to go to the Dark Woods and take the alpha trial. I chose the Paladin people over my own mate.

'You didn't know I would be captured. I didn't know either. There's no sense in living in the past. You got me out.'

My lip quivered and I knew now wasn't the time for this conversation, but I felt so awful that I hadn't been there to support him. Shaking it off, I faced Luka again. "Okay, so what's the plan?"

Over the next hour we devised a plan that accounted

for all the parts that needed to be dealt with. The women and children who were not in fighting shape, the queen, the vampires, fey, and witches occupying Wolf City who needed to be expunged. The trolls that Marmal needed to bring in. All of it. It was like a detailed clock with all the cogs and wheels turning. Everything would need to work for this to be pulled off.

In the end, we had a solid strategy. Marmal left with Pearl to fetch the trolls, and the others departed to do their part.

It was only Luka, Sawyer, and me now.

"Once I kill the queen, will you be king?" I asked Luka. Thinking of ripping her head off gave me satisfaction, but I wanted to know what would happen after, politically.

I wouldn't be opposed to that. He seemed cool, and we could all work together for a more peaceful future between the vampires and werewolves.

He chuckled. "I wish it were that easy. The Drakes are many. The queen is one of sixteen siblings. I have dozens of aunts, uncles, and cousins who will all be vying for the position. Only the most powerful can be crowned, which of course is me."

Of course. Luka wasn't lacking in self-confidence, that was for sure. "How are there that many of you if you can't reproduce with each other?"

His gaze flicked to Sawyer's, and he swallowed hard. Again, I'd touched a nerve.

'*He has a dark past. He's been through a lot,*' was all Sawyer said.

Crap. Now I felt bad. I was about to change the subject when he spoke:

"My family is a legacy family, purebred, obsessed with genetics. That means they stay human and purposefully keep having children and then change us when we reach the age of twenty to forty, freezing time in our bodies forever."

My mouth popped open. Legacy family? I'd never heard of such a thing—wait, so that meant...

"There are human Drakes?" I gasped. They were popping out little Drake vampires like farm animals! It was one of the craziest things I'd ever heard, and also kind of genius if you were concerned with royal lineage.

He just nodded, a deep sadness washing over his features before it was removed by a calm and stoic expression.

"So once the queen dies...?" Sawyer brought both of our attention back to the task, and my cheeks heated with shame that I'd made his friend relive something dark.

"Once the queen dies..." Luka seemed to enjoy the topic change. "There will be a month of mourning. No leadership talk can even happen until that's over. And during that month, all the cousins and uncles and aunts will be trying to assassinate each other so that they can be chosen next."

I sputtered in shock at his words. "That's *quite* the

dysfunctional family," I offered, and then regretted my words.

"You have no idea," Luka said dryly, seemingly unperturbed by my bluntness.

"So you'll hide out in Spokane for the month, take your chance with the hunters?" Sawyer said.

Luka reached up, stretching his arms over his head. "That's the plan."

Were we really doing this? Taking back Wolf City, killing the queen? Could life go back to normal somewhat? I'd been in survival mode for so long, I didn't even know what normal looked like anymore.

"As soon as Marmal gets back with the trolls...we attack," Sawyer announced. "The queen knows we're out of prison. She'll be expecting retaliation, and I don't want to give her the time to plan."

I nodded in agreement. The first war we'd lost because we'd relied too much on technology and guns and helicopters and fancy modern things. All of which the witches had brought down the first day. This time we were smarter, this time we would bring down *their* guns, and fight them with brute pack strength.

CHAPTER TWELVE

Y OU COULDN'T *REALLY* EVER PREPARE FOR WAR. YOU were never *really* ready to risk your life and rush into battle willing to kill someone. There was a deep place inside of all of us, that place where the fight or flight response came from, that prepared you as much as it could, but you had to push yourself the other half of the way. I stood at the open gates of Paladin Village, bringing myself the other half of the way, readying myself for war, where anything was possible.

Marmal had just shown up with over two hundred troll volunteers, all ready to defect from Troll Village, which was currently battling a famine, and live in Wolf City once we restored it. Sawyer had agreed that the future of Wolf City was a shared space where everyone who helped to liberate it was welcome. Witch, troll and werewolf, both Paladin and city, would live in harmony and create a new future that was hopefully unbreakable.

"I'll go in the front lines with the trolls as they disarm the vampires of their technology," Walsh said, snapping me from my thoughts.

Sage and Walsh had been slipping each other awkward glances, and I knew they still hadn't talked about whatever it was that was still between them. Now just wasn't the time.

"Willow and I will accompany the women and children into the bunker," Arrow said, Willow standing beside him with Daisy slung in a cloth pouch around her neck.

Sawyer and I nodded at them both.

Rab stepped forward. "Eugene and I will lead our army behind the trolls and decimate the vampires with fist, teeth, and bow." He grinned, looking feral, and I felt so much pride. My pack was wild and fearsome and unstoppable.

"Sage, Sawyer, Creek, and I will be in the Dark Woods, awaiting the queen's arrival," I said.

It felt slightly cowardly to just go and hide in the woods while a war was being fought, but we'd explained to the pack what our plan was and everyone agreed that if we could just take out the queen, the mastermind, we could end this war. Her son Vicon was dead, her husband the king was dead thanks to Walsh, and if I could bring her down, it would throw the entirety of Vampire City into an uproar. Cause them to mourn and shut down for thirty days just like Luka said. In that thirty days, we would strengthen our borders and secure our land.

"And I," Luka addressed the crowd that stood in front of the Paladin gates, "will lure Bonkers Auntie through Paladin Village and into the Dark Woods, where she will meet her untimely death."

The crowd cheered and I grinned at his term, *Bonkers Auntie.* I had to admit, Luka had grown on me...for a vampire.

"All right, say your goodbyes!" I yelled to the crowd. "We will celebrate when this is all over."

Sawyer nodded. "I owe my wife a proper wedding and you're *all* invited!"

That got some chuckles and cheers. It was amazing how at ease the city wolves were with the Paladins now. Coming here to this land had bonded them and taken the stress off of the two packs who'd been pitted against each other for centuries.

A male city wolf worked his way through the crowd, as warrior women hugged their children goodbye and husbands hugged their pregnant wives.

He looked so familiar but I couldn't place him. It took me a moment. He was the werewolf representative for the freeloaders, or whatever the hell they called themselves.

He tipped his head to me. "We would like to help, if you can use us." He held a samurai sword in one hand and a sharpened spear in another.

Well, well, look who finally had taken a side. Instead of gloating, which I *really* wanted to, I returned the nod. "You and your people can go with Rab and help fight in Wolf City."

He nodded his head in understanding and then disappeared into the crowd, a small contingent of people following him.

Sawyer looked confused so I said, *'I'll tell you later.'*

When I turned, my mother and father were standing there with Sawyer's mom. Creek was asleep in my mother's arms; her eyes were filled with tears. "Are you sure I can't take him with me into the bunker?"

Sawyer shook his head. "We need to stick together. The queen will exploit any weakness, and we can't leave that to chance."

My mom tearily handed Creek over to Sawyer, who slipped him into a sling that Willow had given him. Seeing a shirtless, heavily tattooed male wearing your child was basically the hottest thing ever. Pulling my attention away from my sexy husband and child, I stepped over to my mom and dad and let them pull me into an embrace.

My mom burst into tears, shaking against me as I tried to calm her by patting her back.

"I'll see you in the morning," I told her.

We wanted this to be quick. And whether we won or lost, I thought it would be.

After a lot of tearful goodbyes, Arrow and Willow

set out under the cloak of darkness to hide our people who couldn't fight in the bunker. That was nearly half of our force, but still left us with a little over ten thousand warriors.

As we waited, I started to get nervous about how all the pieces of the puzzle would work.

I pulled Sawyer aside and took in his stressed appearance. He looked tired. His hair was messed up in a cascade of dark strands that fell across his forehead. I could sense the anxiety between our imprint. He wasn't sure this was going to work, and neither was I.

I couldn't be sure of anything anymore, but we had to try.

I reached up and smoothed his hair. "I just wanted to tell you that I love you and you owe me a new wedding ring." I kept it light and he smiled, seemingly grateful that I didn't go too deep or try to say goodbye.

"I love you too, Demi, and I owe you a lot of things." Leaning in, with Creek pressed between us, he placed a kiss to my lips, causing an ache to form in my heart. We'd been through so much together, I just wanted a happily-ever-after. Was that too much to ask?

I was about to say something else when a searing pain sliced up my back and I cried out, falling to my knees.

"Demi!" Sawyer yelled.

I screamed, the pain reaching epic levels as I felt a pull of power from my wolf.

No.

'*I'm so sorry I left you,*' I sobbed as the pain wracked my body in waves. What were they doing to her? I couldn't sense anything but agony.

'*It's...okay,*' she huffed out, and I knew in that moment that the queen had just fed off my wolf. I just knew it.

'*Where are you?*' I asked, sending out my sensations to try to see where she was, but the brief link to my wolf was quickly gone, clamped down as if she'd been torn away. They'd recuffed her. The queen had removed her cuffs, fed on her, and then locked her back up.

"Demi?" Sawyer was on the ground, looking me in the eyes while he cradled Creek with one hand.

I whimpered, wiping my upper lip with the back of my hand. I'd broken out in a cold sweat from the sudden pain.

"I'm okay," I said. "My wolf...the queen fed from her...but I'm okay."

He frowned, not looking as shocked as I expected, and helped me to stand.

I didn't know how she knew, but the queen knew we were on the move. Just like Luka said, she would be "juiced up" on my essence and ready to throw down.

———•·•———

We spent the next half hour getting the mounted warriors onto their steeds and in battle formation. They would be the front line, right after the trolls. I anxiously awaited word from Arrow and Willow, but I didn't want to pry and distract them. Sneaking this many people into Wolf City in the dead of night, when the vampires were most active, was no small feat. If everything lined up right, we would attack at daybreak, when the vampires were weary. Not one of us would sleep tonight. No, our reward of sleep would come tomorrow morning.

If we were still alive.

An hour ticked by and everything was in place. The trolls, the front wave of warriors riding horseback; second wave with spears, bow and arrow; and then the snipers bringing in the rear. We had to assume the witches would use magic to disable the guns, but we were as ready as we would ever be.

Maybe we stood a chance.

'Okay, everyone's in the bunker, awaiting your all clear to come out,' Arrow said.

Relief washed through me. They made it.

'If this goes south, and we lose…if I don't make it and Sawyer doesn't make it…take everyone into Spokane. I don't care what the hunters say.'

He was silent.

'That's an order, Arrow. Everyone to Spokane if this fails. The vampires will lay waste to Paladin lands next. Promise me.'

'Okay. Fine. We go pretend to be human if we lose. Got it,' Arrow countered.

Next, I gave the go-ahead for Marmal and her trolls to move out. Marmal rode Pearl like the badass warrior that she was. They were a sight to behold.

"I want to go with them," I told Sawyer, who stood beside me, rocking on the balls of his heels with Creek on his chest.

"I know. Me too. But we have to focus on the queen. It's what I didn't do before," he said.

The trolls moved quickly into the woods, ready to disarm the vampires. Then Rab and Eugene were standing before us.

"We're ready to follow," Rab told me, thousands of warriors at his back. They stood there, battle ready and wearing expressions of strength and determination.

"I'll bring up the rear," Eugene stated, sitting aloft on a jet-black horse. Gone were the helicopters and Land Rovers. This war would be won the old-fashioned way. The Paladin way.

The horses whinnied as if they could sense the impending conflict.

"Go," I commanded.

'Good luck,' I sent out to my entire pack.

Heads nodded in my direction and then they were off. Rab kicked his horse with his heels and thousands of warriors rushed into the forest.

As Rab and Eugene took off into the woods, the sky started to pinken, throwing swirls of orange as dawn arose.

Something bothered me about hiding in the Dark Woods and leaving it to Luka to be the bait. I wanted to make for damn sure that the queen found me. This whole plan hinged on her.

"Luka, are you sure your aunt will follow you?" I asked. I wanted to kill that woman more than I'd wanted anything in my life.

He shrugged. "Pretty sure."

That wasn't good enough for me. I turned to Sawyer. "Trust me?"

He raised one eyebrow. "Yes…"

I nodded. "Good. I'll be back in a bit. Be ready to roll out when you see me."

He frowned. "I don't want you going anywhere alone."

I looked at the tall vampire covered in tattoos. "I'm not. You're coming with me."

Luka looked surprised, and then at Sawyer as if asking for permission. Sawyer pinned his friend with a glare. "Hit on her and die."

Luka grinned, the points of his teeth extending. "Hey, I look but never touch." He held up his hands in a gesture of submission.

Sawyer's eyes flashed yellow. "*Look* and die."

Luka chuckled, stepping forward and clapping Sawyer on the back. "You alphas and your possessiveness over women, I'll never understand it. You have my word, friend. I'll treat her like she's my sister."

That seemed to calm my husband. Sawyer's eyes flashed back to blue and he gave Luka a curt nod.

Now that the rules had been established, I started to jog out into the forest as Luka zoomed beside me using his vampire speed. "What's the plan, blondie?"

I shook a finger at him. "No flirting!"

He grasped his chest in mock horror. "I'm commenting on your hair color."

"No pet names," I scolded him gently. I wasn't really mad, but I could smell the testosterone and charm coming off of this guy, and it was thick. He'd probably lured hundreds of women with that crap and I had a man, one I was perfectly happy with.

He just gave me a half-cocked smirk, but nodded, keeping pace with my jog easily. "Demi, alpha of the Paladin, what do you require of me?" he asked formally, which only caused me to snort laugh. When I reached the halfway point between Paladin Village and Wolf City, I stopped, catching my breath.

"I'm going to do something, something I know for sure will lure the queen, and then you bring her the rest of the way into the Dark Woods."

He raised one eyebrow, clearly intrigued. "And what is that?"

"I've done this before." I pulled out the tiny sterile needle Raven had given me and pricked my finger, letting a fat drop of blood bead at the tip.

Luka swayed, his nostrils flaring as he grasped the

tree trunk near him. "Dear God, woman, that smells like cotton candy. You're so lucky I just fed."

I just shook my head and reached out, smudging the drop onto the tree trunk Luka held. He leapt backward ten feet, startling me.

"*Don't* wave that liquid heroin in my direction," he growled, his voice predatorial. Maybe I should have thought this through more.

I winced. "Sorry." Squeezing my finger again, I let one more drop form, and then dripped it onto a leaf that rested on the forest floor.

Luka grabbed his mouth. "Holy hell, my mouth is watering. Can we be done with this?"

I tried not to smile but I couldn't help it. Sucking my finger into my mouth, I licked the blood drop off and nodded. "All done. She will come now."

He nodded. "If I don't lick every red blood cell off of that leaf, she will."

"Don't you dare!" I yelled at him.

He rolled his eyes. "I'm kidding. Get out of here. She's fast. She'll only be maybe thirty seconds behind me. Get to the Dark Woods."

He was right. It was time to scram. "Thanks for everything," I told him.

He just pinched his nose shut and waved me away. Ripping off my cuffs, I used my vampire speed to zoom back into camp, where Sage, Walsh, Sawyer, and the baby were waiting.

"Let's go!" I told them, slipping the cuffs back on.

Sawyer picked up the pack we'd filled with things for Creek and we set off with Sage and Walsh beside us at a brisk jog.

Sawyer looked sideways at me. *'Did he flirt?'*

I felt the slight spike of jealousy and had to keep the grin off my face. *'He was a perfect gentlemen.'* When he wasn't lusting after my blood, I wanted to add.

'That would be a first,' Sawyer half chuckled into my mind.

We jogged so fast into the Dark Woods you could almost call it a run. I wanted everyone settled in the cabin before the queen and Luka arrived.

The moment we crossed the threshold of the Dark Woods, Sage whimpered. My eyes snapped to hers and then I followed her gaze.

Damn.

She'd stepped on a nail! There, on the ground, was a piece of wood with a freaking *nail* poking out. The whimper turned into a wail as she pulled her foot up and the nail yanked out of it.

"Holy hell." Walsh moved to help her, but she put out her hand.

"I told you the woods were cursed!" she snapped at him. "And I *don't* need your help. I've done fine on my own this past year."

Walsh's face crumpled in pain, but then he nodded. Okay, that was only slightly awkward. These two were just going to have to have their big fight; otherwise they wouldn't be able to move on.

Sawyer looked down at Creek, who was fast asleep in his little sling on his chest, and placed a kiss on his forehead. Then he pulled the sling over his head and, holding Creek's butt, passed him off to Sage. "Here, maybe if you hold him, the...curse or whatever won't hurt you."

He was right. We'd discovered this over our time here, and it was a nice gesture even though my son was essentially being used as a shield.

She nodded, taking Creek and limping forward. "Let's go!" she snapped, angrier than she probably should be. Her now bleeding foot, Walsh, being back here in the killer woods...I think it was all getting to her.

Sawyer and Walsh followed closely at my side as we ventured farther in. The trees were still in the path I remembered when we'd left, a wide, diagonal, five-foot row that led right to the cabin. They hadn't moved, maybe because I'd shown myself worthy. Whatever the cause, I was grateful. Slipping through the path at a hurried pace, we all stopped when a twig snapped just behind us. Sawyer was bringing up the rear, so when I turned, I was the first to see the giant bear a mere two feet from my mate.

"No!" I snapped, walking right up to the bear and slipping off my cuffs quickly. Now that I had dealt with him twice, I had less fear of him. "They are just here for protection, and will be gone soon. *Don't* harm them." I pushed the compulsion power into my words and the bear took a step backward.

'*Whoa,*' Sawyer said through our bond.

"Go on!" I screamed at the bear. We didn't have time for this.

The bear gave me a long look before he turned, sniffed the ground, and then took off running as I put the cuffs back on.

I spun back around to see Walsh and Sawyer watching me with shocked expressions, while Sage just looked amused.

"I miss the cabin. Come on!" Sage said, and ran with Creek down the rest of the path, limping. The boys shook out of their stupors and followed her. The moment the trees opened up onto the log cabin where I'd spent the last year of my life, I had to swallow down a sob. This cabin had saved my life, my sanity. I had my son here. This was home in a way that was hard to explain.

"Is that it?" Sawyer's voice held a reverence to it. I'd told him all about the cabin. He knew this place was special to me.

I nodded.

He looked impressed. "It's cute."

That brought a smile to my lips, as Sage and I ran giggling to the meadow that held our former home. The tubers she'd been cutting when I'd told her I knew how to get us out of here still lay shriveled on the ground in the same spot.

Slipping into the hut, I looked around and couldn't help but smile at the familiarity. The clay pots, the rabbit fur pelts, Creek's bassinet, everything was so heartbreakingly recognizable.

"You girls lived out here all alone, hunting and fishing and having a baby?" Walsh sounded shocked. Maybe he thought we'd had running water or solar like the Paladin Village.

Sage nodded, pointing to the adjoining room I'd built. "I delivered Creek right in there."

Sawyer moved past us, stepping into the room, and dropped to his knees to press his open tattooed hands onto the flat ground.

"I wish...I could have been there." His voice was growly.

Sage set Creek on my bed and then started to rummage around, arranging the pots how we liked them and cleaning up like it was any old day.

Sawyer suddenly stood, striding over to me, and pulled my face to his with his giant hands. "I can't let anything happen to you or Creek...and I find myself wondering if you can take on the queen yourself."

I frowned. I'd been expecting a pep talk. He didn't believe in me. "You don't think I can?"

Sawyer shook his head. "It's not about that, it's about

the what ifs. What if she's more powerful than you? You said she fed from your wolf. What if she brings twenty vampires? What if they kill us and take Creek?"

Damn. Now he was just scaring me.

I swallowed hard. "I...I have powers—"

"So does she now! She's feasted on your wolf like the bloodsucker she is and now she can do what you can do...and maybe more."

Damn. He was right.

"What do we do? It's too late to retreat or—"

Sawyer pulled my lips close to his, hovering just over them. "Do you trust me?"

"Always." I didn't even hesitate.

"Take off your cuffs," he directed, and I frowned.

Reaching up, I took off my cuffs, ever aware that Sage and Walsh were watching us like hawks. He still held my face in his hands, and the second the cuffs slipped from my wrists, I felt a tug at my power. Fear spiked through me as Sawyer's eyes flashed yellow, and he leaned forward, inhaling.

What the...?

Blue mist, much like that day we first kissed, leaked from my mouth as Sawyer pulled my power into him. It was like he was a vacuum and I was helpless not to be sucked up into his force.

I was so confused about what was happening until it hit me like a ton of bricks. Sawyer was feeding off my essence so that he could help take on the queen. With the two of us sharing this power, we would definitely stand a chance.

I opened myself to him then, as a rush of blue mist lit up his face and his veins glowed with it.

"That's enough!" Sage yelled. "You might weaken her!"

Sawyer broke away, gasping as he looked at his hands as if he didn't recognize them. "Holy shifter, I *feel* it."

"Cuffs on?" Sage, ever the mother figure, rushed to hand them to me.

I shook my head. "Let her come right to me."

It was time to end this war, this hunt, this *queen*. I wasn't going to live the rest of my life being chased across the Magic Lands by this vile hag who was hell-bent on stealing my power.

CHAPTER THIRTEEN

WITH A FINAL KISS GOODBYE, SAWYER AND I LEFT Creek with Walsh and Sage, and then we went to stand just at the edge of the meadow where it touched the trees. Sawyer reached out and took my hand into his and squeezed. We were preparing to take down the queen of the freaking vampires.

"I miss your Instagram posts," Sawyer mused, "your pictures, your silly custom shirts. We have to do this so that things can go back to normal." He gave me a side look and all I saw in it was adoration. "What do you miss?"

I smirked. "First of all, my custom shirts are *not* silly. And secondly, I'll tell you something I don't miss...I don't miss your bare skin. These tattoos are hot." I gave him a sexy wink.

He grinned and opened his mouth to speak when

the trees rustled, and then Luka was suddenly standing before us.

He looked only slightly winded as he gazed at mine and Sawyer's intertwined fingers. "Auntie's coming and she's pissed and powerful." He inhaled the air. "Damn, you both smell good."

My eyes widened at his comment.

Sawyer looked perplexed and Luka shook himself. "Sorry, your powers I meant. It's strong. I can smell it from here."

Sawyer relaxed. "I siphoned some. We'll take down the queen together."

Luka nodded. "Good. Because I can't lay a finger on her without the council saying I tried to help assassinate her."

The leaves on the trees rustled, and then she was standing before us, her dark hair down to her shoulders and windblown. Her sharp cheekbones looked like glass in this early morning light. Five vampire minions fanned out behind her and she grinned, looking feral.

"I *can,* however, help with the entourage," Luka commented, eyeing the five vampire dudes.

"My, my, you've been a pain in my butt." The queen looked right at me, ignoring Luka and Sawyer. "Your wolf though…" She ran her tongue along her sharp teeth. "She's been *so* helpful."

"You hag," I snarled, ready to lunge at her, when Sawyer burst forward. He was vampire-fast, just like me, and the queen was a blur as she advanced to meet him halfway. The second she left the spot where she had been standing, a tree fell behind her, smashing the ground where she'd just been. The land was agitated with all of these people who didn't belong, but now was my chance to help Sawyer take her down.

They collided, Sawyer wasting no time in wrapping his fingers around her throat. I burst forward, meeting her head on, just in time to see her chuck Sawyer out of the way. He slid across the ground and slammed into Luka, who'd bolted forward to take care of the five lackeys.

It was chaos.

Neither of us had guns or even knives, only a few stakes. This was a full-on fistfight. I slammed into the queen, and reaching up, I cracked her chin with my palm, making her teeth crunch together with a satisfying clank. One second I was reaching for her hair and the next I went flying. She'd lashed out with *my* power, sending a force field of some sort right at my chest.

Vile hag.

"Demi!" Sawyer yelled just as I collided with the ground. My back hit first, knocking the breath out of me, and then a deep pain radiated up my spine.

I reoriented myself quickly, standing just in time to see Sawyer crash into the queen, grappling her to the ground. Sage had given Sawyer and I two metal stakes each; they were hidden behind my back in the belt of my pants, which is probably why that fall hurt so much.

Reaching behind me, I pulled one out, just as Sawyer landed a blow to the queen's face. Seeing him hit a woman shook me for a moment, but I had to remind myself this was the woman who kept trying to kill me and had harvested my essence through my wolf.

I zipped forward, stake in hand, and readied myself to come down on her chest with the tip, when I saw a tree move.

"Sawyer look ou—" The words were barely out of my mouth when the tree pounded Sawyer on the back like a nail being driven into wood. One second he was upright, strangling the queen, and the next he was keeled forward over her, knocked out cold.

The trauma of seeing him lifeless made everything feel like it was moving in slow motion. It was so similar to what had happened with Sage, I faltered, nearly tripping over my own feet. After getting my bearings, I rushed forward, just as the queen slipped out from under him and backed away. I let her go, focusing all my attention on my mate.

I could move small things with my mind. I mean, I'd done it with the stake and the queen before, and I needed to get that tree off Sawyer. Reaching out with my power, I wrapped it around the trunk, nearly crying in relief as it lifted, hovering a few inches off of his body. It was wild seeing something suspended in mid-air, and being able to *feel* yourself doing it.

"Get her!" the queen hissed.

My attention was divided as two of the vampires came for me, one from each side. My gaze flicked around the forest to take in the scene. Luka was fighting two others, and one was dead.

These were not good odds. I needed to focus and use all of my strengths. Now was the time to be a badass and really concentrate on everything that made me special.

Taking a deep breath, I fully yanked the tree off of Sawyer, and then hurled it at the two advancing vampires. It slammed into them as they neared me, knocking them over like bowling pins. Sawyer was still unconscious on the ground, but I couldn't worry about that right now. The queen had a maniacal look in her eye, and I didn't know why until it was too late. When Sawyer had fallen, his metal stake had rolled out of his belt strap. The queen had used her newfound power to pick it up with her mind and launch it across the clearing, and I only realized when it lodged in my upper thigh.

A bloodcurdling scream ripped from my throat as the searing pain sliced into the meat of my leg and radiated up into my pelvis. The damn thing was jammed into my thigh at least three inches, and felt like the only thing that had stopped it was my femur bone. Dizziness washed over me at the sight of it and I swayed.

"I'm going to pass out," I mumbled to myself, and then the queen was a blur as she darted for me. One second I was swaying between two trees, and the next

I was in Luka's arms as he ran through the forest, his hands under my knees and behind my back to cradle me to his chest.

"Pass out later, darling. Right now, you need to kill Bonkers Auntie while I help Sawyer." He looked down at me and his nostrils flared as the scent of my blood hit his nose.

He was right. I needed to push through the pain, because he wasn't allowed to kill her or assist in her killing. Clearly, he could still help me, which was good, because I think he'd just saved my life.

He pulled to a stop and I pushed his arm away, forcing myself to stand.

"I got this," I said, deciding to leave the stake in my thigh and not pull it out in case it was plugging a major artery.

"Good luck." He bowed, and then he raced back to where I could see Sawyer still lying motionless on the ground. The one vampire that was still alive was gunning for my man.

Where in the hell was the qu—?

A tree rustled to my right and I spun, ready for her. She tried to reach out and grab me, but I caught her arm and snapped it backward with lethal force.

Her inhuman cry brought me great pleasure as her arm went limp inside of its socket.

"You hag!" she shrieked, grabbing at her dangling arm.

I hissed like a wild cat, right in her face. "I'll tear you limb from limb if I have to."

She reached behind her back with her good arm and pulled something out. The glint of metal caught my eye. I thought it was another stake until I saw that it was two half circles, connected on one side.

It was a damn collar. Electric no doubt.

Oh hell no.

I felt my power rise up inside of me, like a live wire just under my skin, and I latched on to it in that moment, wrapping it around myself, and then around the queen. It was hard to explain, but I felt these invisible threads reach out and clasp on to her like glue. Her eyes went wide, so I knew she felt it too. An invisible burst of energy blasted from her as she tried to protect herself. It slammed into me, but I held on to her with my magic threads. The wind knocked from my chest, leaving me gasping, but I stayed standing, pulling her slowly toward me.

She flailed, a genuine look of panic on her face as her toes scraped across the dirt, dragging bits of leaves and moss with her as I lured her into my web like a spider. Holding one of the stakes Sage had given me, I raised it, grinning as she was brought to me.

"No!" she shouted, pushing another shock wave of energy into me. It slammed into my solar plexus and I could no longer stay upright. I tumbled backward, my sticky energy web of power bringing her down with me.

We landed awkwardly, with her falling onto the lower half of my good leg as we tumbled, grappling with each other.

I grabbed anything I could, a fistful of hair and her left ear, yanking her face toward me so that she didn't slither away. She opened her mouth, hissing, and then jerked out of my grasp, sinking her teeth into the meat of my uninjured thigh.

A chunk of her hair was left in my hand and I recoiled at the pleasureful sensation of her bite.

The hag was refueling.

Nope. Not today.

Reaching out, I punched her in the side of the head, dislodging her teeth from my skin before she could drink from me. She rolled to the side and then scrambled onto her knees, trying to get on top of me. I tried to right myself, but my injured thigh and the pain it was causing me was slowing me down. Before I knew it, she knocked me back down and hovered over me with a feral, bloody grin. "My lead scientist thinks that if I just drain you fully, your powers will transfer to me permanently. I say we try that now. I'm not sure you're worth the trouble of keeping alive."

I planted my booted foot right on her chest. "I say we don't!" With as much strength I could muster, I kicked, chucking her off of me, and she went flying. Her scream of frustration cut deep into the woods as she landed with a loud thud in the trees.

I stood shakily, readying myself for her to come at

me again. This was harder than I thought, but I was determined to end this now and not retreat, nor let her withdraw.

I pressed on, limping forward, stalking through the trees. Trying to inject some vampire speed into my run, I leapt over a fallen log, wincing when the pain shot up my leg and I had to slow down.

Where was she?

I didn't kick her this far. Did she leave? Was she going to come back with an army? I trusted Sage and Walsh to protect Creek, but something told me she was still here, watching me and waiting.

"Come on, you coward!" I screamed, feeling the full-blown rage of every pain she'd cause me come to the surface.

A tree rustled and I spun, eyeing the queen, who stood just behind a tree in an effort to camouflage herself. But I also saw something else, something she didn't see. The giant bear that had been such a pain in my butt stood just behind her, sniffing the air.

She must have smelled him, or felt him, because she turned, her eyes widening just as he opened his mouth, showcasing his massive teeth and let loose a terrifying roar. The queen charged forward, toward me and away from the bear, but I wasn't going to let her get away. With what little strength I had left, I burst forward, ignoring the pain in my thigh, and grasped her shoulders. Kicking off the ground, I pushed her backward into the bear.

This fall wouldn't hurt me; this bear wouldn't hurt me—we were one, family, on the same side. I knew this. The bear reared up on his hindlegs, making himself terrifyingly tall, and the queen slammed right into his chest.

"*Attack!*" I threw compulsion into my command.

Without even a second's delay, he reached for her with his paws and trapped her against his chest, tearing into her abdomen like it was Play-Doh. Her wails of agony ripped from her throat and I backed up, wincing at the gore before me. Throwing her to the ground, he pounced on her chest, and the sound of cracking bones filled the forest.

Oh God.

When he bit into her shoulder, I pulled the stake from behind my back. Dragging my bum leg across the forest floor, I bent down before her, the bear keeping her pinned to the spot as she grabbed at him weakly, trying to throw him off. He must weigh over a thousand pounds and she was too injured to fight him. This was the end for her.

"This is for everyone you tortured in your pursuit of power. Say hi to Vicon in hell for me." Then I slammed the tip of the stake right into her heart.

A final gurgled scream left her throat and then cut off mid-yell. Black veins crawled up her neck as her body decomposed into ash, first turning into a crusted shell of skin and then becoming powder.

The bear backed up, looked at me and then took

off. Either he was freaked out by her decomposing or he figured his work here was done. He'd rid the sacred forest of her threat.

I stared at the pile of ashes, numb to the realization that I'd actually done it.

I killed her. *It's over.*

Reaching out, I brushed my fingers against the black ash, rubbing some between my fingers as if I couldn't believe this was real.

The queen of the vampires, the mother of my rapist, the woman who tortured Seam's daughter, stole my wolf, tried to kill my husband, and brought war to our people...was dead.

My throat constricted with emotion as the tightness in my chest finally released and I felt like I could breathe for the first time in so, so, long.

"I'm here!" Sawyer called out, and I spun to see him holding two stakes, one in each fist, blood and bruises covering his shoulders and the side of his neck.

I shook my head, indicating the pile of ashes on the ground as the tears spilled over and I quickly wiped them away with the back of my hand.

"I took care of it," I told him, my voice vacant. I still felt empty, unfinished, and I didn't realize why until I remembered that I didn't have my wolf. This wasn't over until I got my wolf back. Where the hell was she?

"While you were napping, your girl killed the most powerful queen the vampires have ever seen." Luka strolled up and patted Sawyer on the back. "How does that feel?"

Sawyer flipped him off and I shook my head at Luka before looking down at my thigh and wincing at the horrible sight.

"They hurt, huh?" Luka stared at the stake protruding out of my thigh. Then he lifted his shirt to showcase over fifty puckered scars all around his chest and abdomen. I hadn't noticed them before…

My mouth dropped open. "You've been staked that many times?"

He grinned, and holy hell he was super good-looking. If Sage and Walsh didn't figure their crap out, I might just be okay with her hooking up with a vamp. Or I'd have to set up Raven with him.

He nodded. "It will leave a scar, but you'll heal."

Sawyer dropped his stakes to the ground and pushed forward, yanking me into his arms. He tucked me into his chest, wrapping his arms around me, and I took in a deep breath. "Let's get you back to medical. Dr. Pearson can work on this," Sawyer mumbled against the top of my head as he held me.

I nodded, reaching up to stroke his beard as I pulled back from him a little so that I could look him in the eyes. "Sawyer…my wolf. I can't feel her. I…need her back."

He frowned, nodding. "I'll figure it out."

With that, we headed back to the cabin, where I

found Creek safe with his auntie, and hopefully uncle by the way Walsh was looking at Sage. Luka had to dodge a few falling trees, but we all made it out, the trail still leading us to the Paladin lands, just as it had when I'd opened the cave and proved myself. Sawyer insisted on carrying me, and I looked over his shoulder the entire way, watching the cabin get smaller and eventually fade into the distance.

I would miss this place. As screwed up as that sounded, it was true.

———•·•———

Once back in Paladin Village, Luka said goodbye and left for Spokane to hide out as the month of mourning for the queen would begin. Because the queen had been the one to lead the war against the wolves and essentially forced the other races into it, now that she was dead, none of them had come forward to continue the war. We'd won.

Sawyer left me with Dr. Pearson and then went to publicly declare the war was over and officially take our land back. The trolls' magic had worked beautifully, and we'd pushed their forces all the way back to the eastern wall. Luka said the vampires would feel their queen die and he was right. Once they did, their army had surrendered and went into mourning, back in their city.

Dr. Pearson gave me some really good drugs. I was

in and out as the one-inch hole in my leg healed with a little help from skin glue and stitches. Astra was asleep in the bed next to me.

Sawyer stopped by when I was lucid and told me that our people came up out of the bunker and now the planning would begin. We'd have defector trolls, witches, and two types of wolves living in Wolf City, but we wouldn't want it any other way. This was how it should have always been.

I felt the heaviness of sleep pull on me just as Sawyer was telling me about his plan to repair and rebuild Wolf City. Right before I closed my eyes, I felt her. My wolf. She was alive, injured but okay, and someone had just removed a magical collar from her.

'*Where are you!?*' I screamed, trying to jump to her sight so that I could see where she was, but the drugs were too heavy.

'*With the Magical Creature Council. They're coming, and they want both you and Sawyer in prison. You need to run.*'

Oh crap. It was the last thought I had before I slipped into a drugged oblivion.

CHAPTER FOURTEEN

I AWOKE WITH THE EARLY MORNING LIGHT, THE GROGGI-
ness of the medicine receding as I opened my eyes.
Sawyer's blue gaze was the first thing mine landed on.

"Hello, my love." He leaned forward, propping his
elbows on the edge of my bed and stroking my hair.

"Creek?" I asked, my eyes adjusting to the light.

"He's fine. With your mom and my mom getting
grandma time." His voice was rough like he'd just
awoken as well.

I looked to the left and saw the bed empty.

"Astra!" I sat upright so fast I almost cracked into
Sawyer's nose, the pain in my thigh throbbing with the
sudden motion.

Sawyer held out his hands. "Whoa, whoa. She's
okay. She's on a light walk with Willow to regain her
strength."

I relaxed a little, wondering why I was so jumpy. The queen was dead, we'd gotten our land back, everything was fi—

'*Run!*' My wolf's voice burst through the final remnants of my hazy mind and the memory of what she'd said last night came back to me.

"Sawyer! We need to run, the Magical Creature Council has my wolf. They want us in prison and they're coming."

Sawyer's eyes widened into saucers. "What?"

I jumped up from the bed, swaying, just as I heard the commotion outside. Murmurs, yelling, and a familiar howl.

My wolf.

It was too late.

Sawyer and I scrambled outside to see what all the commotion was about, and I froze when I saw my wolf, tethered with a collar and leash like a damn dog. My gaze ran along the chain to look into the eyes of a tall, lithe dark fey. He wore a long, black fitted trench coat that skimmed the ground, and he stood next to five other people. One from each race.

The Magical Creature Council.

My gaze darted to each person. Troll woman, light fey male, witch female wearing a black crushed velvet cape, a dark fey male, a stout male werewolf I didn't recognize, and a towering male vampire.

They were an ominous sight, all of the races walking

together like this, knowing that half hated the other. The Paladins and Ithaki had no representation, which I wasn't surprised by.

"Let. Her. Go." My voice could have cut glass. I would kill every single one of them for chaining her like that.

The witch woman raised her hand and then snapped. A silver collar flew out of nowhere then, latching around my neck and closing with a click.

What the…!

She did the same to Sawyer beside me, and then we were both brought to our knees against our will.

Who was this woman? She looked barely twenty-five, with dark black hair and cherry red lips, but her power…it was unheard of.

The witch held up her hand, as if controlling us like puppets.

I reached up to yank off the collar and got the shock of my life. The sharp sting zapped into my neck, causing me to cry out.

Our pack went wild then. Paladin and city wolf pressed forward. The sound of bones cracking signaled their shifting. Screams of anger were hurled at the council as they threw themselves forward. But when they got too close, a bubble-like shield erected from the witch woman, covering us, my wolf, and the council, and no one else. It was instantaneous, thick like glass, and I felt myself marveling at this councilwoman's incredible power. When the pack slammed against the shield, they too were zapped with electricity.

"Stop!" I cried to our people, not wanting anyone to get hurt on my account. Then I looked to the witch. Only a high priestess would have this kind of power, and Raven had told me that you didn't make high priestess at that age unless you were a magical prodigy.

"Sawyer Hudson and Demi Calloway-Hudson, you are hereby under arrest for the recent jailbreak from Magic City Prison and your role in the crime. You have the right to an attorney and trial hearing. You may opt to forgo lengthy legal proceedings and enter into a quick and instant trial right here and now."

I frowned, looking at Sawyer. Her power...her human lie detector power that Star had told me about, this is what she was referencing.

'She'll see everything, and she'll show everyone here, like a movie playing out from your memory,' Sawyer warned.

I nodded. "I will consent to an instant trial right now about the jailbreak, but only if you promise to reopen Sawyer's murder case, take my testimony, and look at *everything*."

I had to bite my lip to keep from crying. Showing her and everyone here my rape would be one of the most horrific things I'd ever had to relive, but if it would save Sawyer, I would do it.

Her brows drew together. "You know of my abilities

and you would consent to have me see that you master-minded a jailbreak?"

I nodded. "If you would *also* see that Vicon Drake raped me when I was fifteen."

Every council member inside of the bubble gasped.

"Lies!" the vampire councilmen roared. "What a convenient little falsehood to save her beloved. Cry rape. How *original*," he seethed.

I could see the veins in the witch's neck twitch. She didn't like him.

"Is she crying rape if she's willing to allow my power to see the truth?" the witch spat at him, looking up at the vampire with a cold gaze.

He just puckered his lips, like he'd sucked on something sour.

"I will grant your request. Consider his case reopened." The witch stepped closer to me, extending her hand, and I froze.

I had only flashes of memory from that night. I didn't want to see the whole thing, to remember more. Sensing my anxiety, my wolf bucked against the collar and the chain went taut in the witch's hand.

'*I have the memories. Let me do it,*' she said.

It dawned on me then, she was right. *She* was the one who'd saved me and locked everything away to protect me.

'*Are you sure?*' I asked.

She nodded.

"Let my wolf join me, and then I'll show you. She has the memories of that night. The night my soul split in two," I added, and glared at the male vampire.

At my request, compassion crossed the faces of the witch, troll, and light fey.

"I'll allow that, but if you try *anything*, I'll kill him instantly." The witch pointed to Sawyer and the dark fey broke out of formation to stand behind my mate.

Sawyer peeled his lips back, growling, but didn't move.

The young witch councilwoman walked over to my wolf and unlatched the cuff at her neck. The second it fell to the ground, I dropped to my knees and opened my arms. Tears lined my eyes as she leapt into the air, going spectral, and slammed into my chest. I burst into sobs as she filled me up, making me feel whole and normal and sane for the first time since I'd left her.

'*Never again. I'm so sorry,*' I told her, hugging my chest.

'*It's okay,*' she promised. '*We can get through anything.*'

I looked up into the surprised faces of the council, wiping the tears from my cheeks. Why did everyone look so shocked? It's like they hadn't really expected her to join me. Maybe they thought my split shifting was a rumor and she was a decoy pack wolf or something. Shaking herself from her stupor, the witch held out her hand again.

"Do I, Callie Heartstone, have your permission to

enter your mind and see all there is to see pertaining to the truth?" she asked.

Enter my mind? I wanted to cry out, *Hell no*, but I knew the truth was the only way out of this mess. "I do," I told her, and then turned to Sawyer. "Promise me you won't look." My lower lip shook and his entire face fell. It was like I'd just stabbed him. You could see the pain play across his features.

'Promise me,' I pushed through our imprint, relieved to find that the collar didn't keep me from mentally speaking to my mate. I couldn't live the rest of my life with this man if I knew that he'd seen the darkest night of my soul play out like a movie.

I just couldn't. Some things needed to stay private in a marriage, and this was a deal breaker for me.

He swallowed hard, his eyes flashing yellow. "I promise." His voice broke.

"Okay, very cute," the vampire councilman sneered at Sawyer and me. "Let's get this over with so we can lock them up."

The witch's nostrils flared in irritation, and then she looked at me, softening her gaze. "Show me your memory of the night of the alleged incident with Prince Vicon Drake."

Alleged. That was such a hurtful word to someone telling the truth.

I reached out to touch her hand, at the same time that I turned and faced Sawyer.

The left wall of the dome we were in lit up like a movie screen and there was fifteen-year-old me and Raven getting out of a car and laughing as we walked up to Vicon's house, where music could be heard inside.

Wow.

Her abilities were...incredible. She'd pulled my memory from my brain and then projected it on the wall with sound and color and everything.

"Hello, beautiful ladies." Vicon opened the door with a bottle of beer and a handsome smile. This was my memory, and I felt that my wolf was about to take over and show hers. Flicking my eyes from the screen, I looked into the deep blue eyes of my mate. He was staring at my face and making an effort not to look at the screen beside him.

'I love you,' I said as Vicon's pick-up lines played out in the background.

'I love you so much more.' Sawyer reached up, shielding my peripheral vision with his hands. *'Everything about you. Even this.'*

I whimpered at his words, and then my fifteen-year-old scream cut through the space.

Fifteen-year-old me said no. I said no *four* damn times, but Vicon kept going, his friend's voices joining him, egging him on. There were grunts, moans, shrieks, but I blocked them all out and just looked into my future, letting my past go up in flames. I didn't live there anymore. I refused to.

'Each day gazing into her blue eyes is like looking into the ocean. You come to learn there is endless depth,' Sawyer said.

I couldn't help but give him a weak smile as we blocked out the growling and the noise of fists smacking bone. The witch gasped and so did some of the Paladins behind the bubble, but I just focused on my mate. The one who believed me when I'd said what Vicon did and demanded justice for it.

'Who wrote it?' I asked. He was always spouting poetry to me. It was one of the ways he wooed me at our time in Sterling Hill.

Sawyer stroked my cheek. *'I did.'*

My fifteen-year-old wolf's howl cut into the bubble from the screen and the witch clapped her hands. "I think we've seen enough." Her voice shook with emotion.

I had to take a few deep breaths to calm myself, keeping my eyes on Sawyer and just feeling the sorrow from my wolf before I could pull away and finally face the council.

Each and every one of them stared at their feet, all except the witch. She boldly met my gaze.

"She was telling the truth." Her voice held pride and I had to swallow hard to keep from crying.

"Doesn't change the fact that she broke out five high-value prisoners," the vampire mumbled, head still down.

The witch looked absolutely stricken. "Of course it

does! She's the mate and wife of the alpha! When Vicon Drake stole her virginity, he soiled her for the future alpha, violating Section 5A of the Magical Creature Code. Sawyer Hudson was well within his right to kill him and seek redemption for his future mate's purity. Which means Sawyer was wrongly imprisoned. And also means Demi was within her right to free her mate when justice failed them both."

Holy snakebite. I mean, I didn't love the words *soiled* and *purity*, but she was kind of a badass with all that section 5A stuff. This woman should be a lawyer.

"I vote to absolve both of them of their crimes and get back to our day!" the witch called out. "All in favor, say—"

"Hang on a minute," the dark fey sneered. "I agree she was well within her right to free her mate, but what of the other four felons? They were not to be freed, and she should be held accountable for that!"

My eyes flicked to the outside bubble, where Walsh and Sage stood anxiously, peering in at us. *'Tell Walsh to run,'* I told Sage calmly. The dark fey had a point, and I wasn't sure what was going to go down now. Sage nodded slowly, grabbing Walsh by the arm and yanking him into the crowd.

The dark fey followed my gaze, but they'd gotten away in time. I glared at him, about to speak in my defense, when the witch opened her mouth. "You saw the security footage. They all jumped on the dragon and escaped themselves, she didn't *force* them. As far as I am concerned, they are still fugitives, and when we find them we will prosecute them to the full extent of the law. Demi and Sawyer Hudson are innocent. All in favor, say aye!"

Sawyer reached out and took my hand.

'If this goes badly, I'll charge them, and you break out of the bubble and run. Go to the Dark Woods and take Creek. You will be safe there.'

'No,' I told him.

'Dammit, Demi! Can't you just do what I say for once in your life?'

Nope.

'Fine,' I lied.

"Aye," the dark fey said. "*If* we hunt down the other fugitives."

The witch rolled her eyes at the dark fey's comment. "Aye." She looked to the troll councilwoman.

"Aye." The troll tipped her head in my direction and then stared at the light fey.

"Aye." Then the light fey glanced at the vampire.

"Nay," he seethed, eyeing both Sawyer and me.

The witch shook her head at the vampire. "Majority rules. They are now freed of all crimes against them."

Cheers erupted outside the bubble, and Sawyer relaxed beside me. The witch snapped her fingers and both collars fell from our necks.

We...we were free. The protection bubble popped

around us and the witch councilwoman stepped forward, bowing slightly. "I'm sorry for the inconvenience."

Hah. That was the understatement of the year. But if I hadn't gone to the Dark Woods for so long, and I'd been able to testify at Sawyer's hearing, we probably could have avoided all of this.

I gave her a nod and she made her way out of the crowd, the rest of the council following her as the pack parted with glares and growls.

Turning to face me, Sawyer pulled my face to his and pressed a firm kiss on my lips.

"Marry me," he breathed.

I laughed. "I already did!"

He pulled back and gazed at me. "A real wedding, with our son and every person alive watching. We'll televise it for all to see. I want big. Huge. Celebrity worthy."

I grinned. "Our venue got blown up, and most of Wolf City is in ruins. I'm pretty sure fancy is out of the question."

He looked around Paladin Village, out at the cornfield and the giant weeping willow that was nestled in the meadow. "We'll get married here."

My throat tightened with emotion and the rightness of that statement, and I nodded as a single tear ran down my cheek. This man right before me was the best life partner I could have ever dreamed of.

I couldn't wait to grow old with him. Together, we

would lead my people, his people—our people. This pack would grow into one pack, and become the most powerful werewolf pack the world had ever seen, and we would never fall prey to a takeover again. Mark my words.

EPIL⊙GUE

N O, PUT THEM IN THE CENTER!" WILLOW CALLED
to a pack member who was setting a centerpiece
at one of the hundreds of tables that sat in the meadow
beyond the cornfield. I'd just married Sawyer in the little
Paladin church. People had packed the space and then
spilled out into the town. I'd walked down the aisle
holding Creek, before handing him off to my mom. And
it was perfect.

It had been two weeks since we'd won the war. Walsh
had to escape into Spokane and stay with Luka for a bit
to lay low, but they all said they would risk it and come
for the wedding. I looked now at Sawyer standing by
the outdoor open bar we'd set up. He leaned against
it, handing out shots from the bartender to his boys.
Walsh, Luka, Bennett, and Talon, they all made it.

The sun set deeper into the skyline as the white

Christmas lights flicked on and lit up the meadow. The boys pounded their shots and then asked for another, getting louder by the moment. I grinned, pretty sure I was the only one sober right now.

"You know my favorite part of this amazing wedding?" Sage said.

I turned to face my redheaded bestie. She pointed and I followed her gaze with a mischievous grin on my face. Meredith sat at one of the dining tables, two wolf security guards standing behind her to make sure she didn't run. She scowled at the cornfields and sipped on her glass of water as the silver cuffs on her wrists glinted in the moonlight. I'd invited her mother too, but she couldn't come on account of the fact that Sawyer had found her alive and well and living in hiding with the vampires and then had her imprisoned.

"I can't believe you put her in the front row at church. I thought Meredith was going to leap forward and strangle you to death."

My grin grew wider. "Front row too petty?"

Sage tipped her head back and laughed. "Not at all."

Did I care? No. Meredith was forced to watch me marry Sawyer in front of everyone, and after she and her mother tried to ruin our relationship, she deserved a lot worse.

I glanced to Marmal, who was chatting up Talon and totally flirting. It was so nice to see that she was happy here. I'd put her in charge of the stables, and we were building Pearl her own giant barn. Not many people could say they had a dragon in their pack, but I did. Pearl and Marmal were bonded in a way, and a package deal. My gaze then bounced to Astra. She'd fully healed and was now dancing with a younger teenage Paladin male named Steel. He was a good guy, though I suddenly felt protective over Astra as his hands went lower on her hips.

"Let her have fun. Party kill," Sage snapped.

I scoffed. "I am not."

Sage just shook her head. "Astra is your favorite. Everyone knows."

I shrugged. "That's true."

Sage's mouth opened in shock and she smacked me in the shoulder. "How dare you? I'm supposed to be your favorite."

I burst into laughter, about to say more, when Sage's face lit up with surprise as she looked at someone behind me. So many people had been coming through to send their congratulations on their way to their table that I expected a wedding guest. When I spun to see who had made her so stunned, I saw a troll-fey Ithaki walking toward me. He wore a black top hat and a dingy old tuxedo with dust on the pant legs and patches on the elbows, but he looked handsome.

"Seam?" I was shocked he'd come. I hadn't invited him—not that I was mad he was here. I had mailed him the queen's ashes, just as promised, so he'd probably gotten it by now. Maybe he was here to thank me, which was really sweet, especially since he'd attempted to dress up.

I felt Sawyer bristle over at the bar and step toward me, but I put my hand out.

'*Who's that Ithaki?*' Sawyer growled.

'*It's Seam. The guy who helped me get you out.*'

Sawyer relaxed, probably staring at the dude with awe. Seam was a big deal in Magic City Prison.

Seam tipped his hat to me, his pointed ears sticking out of the side. "I don't want to interrupt your big night, but I got your package." He grinned and it caused me to beam. "When I heard in town that you were having a wedding, I just had to come give you a present."

He held out his hand to me, something in his fist, and my heart beat frantically in my chest.

Seam got me a present.

I offered him my flat palm and my engagement ring plopped into it.

"I couldn't sell it. Varilla wouldn't want me to. You keep it and be happy, okay?"

My throat tightened as I nodded, blinking back tears. "I'll send you the money for it. I'll buy it from you—"

He waved me off. "You've given me more than money could ever buy," he said, and then tapped his chest. "You've given me peace. Knowing that monster is dead and not hurting anyone else."

He tipped his hat again and bowed. "I must get back to my roses," he said before walking away back into the crowd.

"You can stay!" I shouted after him but he merely lifted his hand and waved me off before disappearing into the forest.

My head slowly spun to Sage, to see she was wiping away tears.

"We totally underestimated that dude," Sage said.

I nodded, blotting my eyes. "Damn." I blew air through my teeth and watched him fully disappear into the trees as I slipped the ring back on my finger. I looked over at Sawyer, who was watching me keenly.

'Did he just give you the ring back?' He sounded confused.

I nodded, still overcome with emotion and then smiled at Sawyer from across the garden. My little felon looked sexy in a tuxedo.

Luka pounded his tenth shot and slammed the empty glass onto the bar top. Then he grabbed Sawyer's hand and thrust it into the air. "One woman for life!" Luka screamed, causing me and Sage to shake our heads, laughing. Prison had changed these boys, they were wild and rowdy and unpredictable, and I liked it.

Sage continued to shake her head. "He's a wild card, that one."

I giggled, enjoying the little bro-fest Sawyer was

having. He'd missed his friends while they were hiding out in Spokane. They had such a close bond.

"So's *that* one." I pointed to Walsh, who had the shot glass poised to his lips as he stared at Sage over the top, his eyes burning yellow. "Have you guys talked?" I pressed her.

She sighed. "Yep. He told me he wanted to date, he's *finally* ready."

"That's great!" I said. "But why don't you sound excited and why is he glaring at us?" I asked her, unnerved by Walsh's gaze.

She looked at me, chewing on her bottom lip. "He's a wanted felon, jumping around with Luka and hiding with the humans in Spokane. I'm your second-in-command. I can't follow him around the country—"

I put a hand up to her face. "Wait, he asked you to go live with him and you said no because of duty? Are you *bonkers?*" I shook a finger in my bestie's face. "That's as bad as what he used to do when he wouldn't give your relationship a try because of his responsibilities to Sawyer."

"Yeah, well, payback sucks!" she growled, her eyes going yellow.

I shook my head. "You're not like that though, Sage, and you love him. I can smell it."

She burst out laughing and rolled her eyes. "You can't smell love."

I shrugged playfully. "Sure I can. It smells like

sunshine, roses, and…" I looked around and spied the chocolate fountain our guests were dipping strawberries into. "…and chocolate."

She shook her head, but she was grinning from ear to ear. "I don't smell like that."

"But you *do* love him. Right?" I knew she did. Out in the Dark Woods we'd had the most honest conversations two people could have. Sage loved him. He was the one for her.

She glanced at Walsh, who hadn't moved; he'd gone full-on stalker mode, just staring at her. "Of course I do. It's Walsh." She sounded mad, like she wanted to stop it but couldn't.

I nodded, taking in a deep breath. "Rab!" I yelled over the crowd where he was dancing with Daisy. He snapped to attention and walked over, holding his baby girl on his hip. Reaching out, I placed one hand on either of Sage's shoulders. "Sage Hudson, you are relieved of duty as my second-in-command."

Her mouth popped open and I could feel the hurt flash across our bond as she stared at me in shock. I swiveled my head to the left, just as Rab walked up. "Rab, you're my new second."

He looked surprised, glancing from Sage to me before breaking out into a grin. "Position accepted. Thank you, Alpha." He bowed and walked away.

"You can't do that!" Sage snapped, shrugging out of my grasp.

"You forget I am a true alpha, connected with you through a pack bond. I *feel* you pining over him."

She covered her chest, glaring at me. "It will go away when he goes away."

I chuckled. "That's not how it works, and what if he shows up next time with a new girl?"

Her eyes flashed yellow as her teeth clenched. "I'd kill her."

I tipped my head back and laughed. "Sage. Sister. Best friend. Go. Say *yes*."

Her arms fell to her sides and she seemed to consider it. Pulling her bottom lip into her mouth, she chewed on it for a moment, tossing the idea around in her head. Then she looked up at Walsh.

He was still watching her.

"He's a wanted felon," she griped.

I nodded. "And Sawyer and I will be working to clear him of that charge. I'm sure we can dig up crimes on the Vampire King."

She looked wistful. "I mean, I have always wanted to live in the human world for a bit."

I nodded. "Do it. Go to Liberty Lake, there is a boba tea shop there called BocoPop. Get the oolong milk tea with cheese foam. You won't regret it."

She scrunched up her face. "Cheese foam? That sounds horrifying."

I laughed. "It's amazing. Come on, Sage. Follow your heart."

She heaved a big sigh and then turned to face Walsh, who was still watching her like a lovesick puppy dog.

She put one finger out and pulled it toward her, beckoning him.

He set down his full shot glass, eyes lighting up a fiery orange, like the evening sun. Taking long strides, he crossed the lawn and made his way to her. He wore a dark gray tuxedo and had never looked more handsome. Sage's deep green, skintight dress clung to her athletic form, and her hair was in a cascade of curls hanging loosely over one shoulder. If I had my camera with me, I'd have taken a picture of this moment. Walsh walked right up to her and grabbed her, dipping her backward as he cradled the back of her neck. Then he kissed her, a movie style kiss. A-holy-hell-is-this-really-happening-in-real-life-kiss. I smiled, happy for their tender moment, and Raven walked up beside me.

"Damn…I wanna be kissed like that," she said.

I eyed Luka who was definitely tipsy. Werewolves were easy to get drunk, but vampires less so. "Come on, I'll introduce you to someone, but I can't promise it will be more than one night."

Raven followed my gaze and her eyes glittered. "Oh, I'll take one night of that."

We both hooked arms and giggled as we passed Sage and Walsh, who were now full-on making out in full view of my wedding party.

I approached Sawyer and he spun, eyeing me with a

look of absolute passion. My dress was a fully blinged-out, expensive number that Sage talked me into. There were more crystals and beads on this thing than there were werewolves in the entire world. But I loved it, and I felt beautiful in it.

"Luka..." I approached the vampire. "Have I introduced you to one of my bestest friends in the world?" I held up Raven's hand and she spun, her tight black velvet dress catching the last of the dying sun's rays as it accentuated her curves. "This is Raven."

Luka's eyes glittered, his nostrils inhaling as he was no doubt smelling what supernatural race she was.

He gripped his glass of whiskey and gave her a devastatingly handsome grin. "I have always had a thing for witches. Dance with me?" He set his drink down and stepped forward, holding out his hand.

Raven beamed, placing her hand in his, and they stepped out onto the dance floor.

Sawyer faced me then, and holy hell on wheels was he sexy in his black tuxedo. His neck tattoos were sticking out just above the collar and his eyes absolutely smoldered as they looked at me.

"What are you thinking about right now?" I asked as he took me into his arms.

He gave me a devilish grin, reaching out to cup my waist. "Where the zipper to this dress is."

A genuine laugh pealed out of me as he spun me around, and I sighed in contentment. Reaching out, he stroked the cuffs at my wrists. They were a new wedding set, encrusted with diamonds and pearls, at my request. We might have won the war, but I didn't trust that history wouldn't repeat itself. For now, I was going to fly under the radar and just enjoy my life with my beautiful family.

"Wife?" Sawyer gazed down at me tenderly.

"Yes, husband?"

"Let's have five more babies." Sawyer grabbed my chin and pulled me into him, planting a sweet kiss on my lips as I barked out a laugh.

Okay, clearly he *was* drunk because I was closing up shop after two more. Max. But I loved our life and I was excited for our future. We'd started to run this pack as one big family. Sometimes I took a city wolf issue and sometimes he took a Paladin issue, but mostly we kept to our previous packs when being in charge. It would all take time, we just had to figure out where we were going to live…a conversation for another day.

"Are you ready for your wedding gift?" Sawyer grinned.

"You got me a wedding gift? Damn, I suck, I didn't get you anything." I winced. I was so bad at this kind of stuff.

Sawyer waved me off and walked over to my mom, who was holding Creek. Taking our son, he brought him over to me and beckoned me toward a lantern-lit pathway that disappeared into the forest.

"Sawyer, we can't leave our wedding. Where are you going?" I whisper-screamed.

He turned a corner and the path wound to an open… parking lot? My eyes widened at the sight of the freshly laid gravel parking lot; it was *full* of electric scooters, like the ones from Wolf City.

Sawyer spun. "I cleared it all with Rab and Arrow. We replanted the trees, and the scooters are electric and solar powered so nature wasn't harmed." He pointed to a baby pink one with a little side car on it that had a car seat inside. I grinned.

"Is that for me and Creek?" Tears welled in my eyes.

Sawyer nodded. "This thing clocks thirty miles per hour. I timed it and it's only nine minutes to the edge of Wolf City, where we can build one of two homes." He gestured to the new paved path that led into the forest. There'd been a road between our two territories, and he'd essentially joined them as one and it meant the world to me.

The tears spilled over and my chest felt tight as Sawyer planted a kiss on Creek. "One home there and our little cottage here. We will split the time, fifty-fifty."

I was too choked up to say anything more. Sawyer reached out and grabbed a pink helmet, slipping it over my head.

"What? No, Sawyer, our wedding!" I fussed as he clipped it under my chin and then strapped Creek into his car seat sidecar.

"We'll be back in twenty minutes to cut the cake. Everyone is too drunk to notice we are even gone." He assured me as he stepped over to a matte black scooter.

I grinned. This man and his romantic gestures.

"Twenty minutes! And I better not have helmet hair after."

Sawyer's lips curled into a smirk and then he took off on his scooter as I turned mine on and followed after him. The paved road was a smooth and beautiful ride through the stunning thickly treed Paladin forest. My gaze kept flicking to Creek to see that he'd fallen asleep in his little car seat. The path was well lit and sure enough, in under ten minutes we approached the edge of Werewolf City.

Zipping out onto the road, I followed Sawyer as he took a left, toward the ruins of what used to be Sterling Hill.

Just as I was wondering if it was really necessary to take us on a tour of the destruction of Werewolf City during our wedding, I saw the giant construction cranes moving panels of glass and metal sheet roofing as they rebuilt the school.

He'd started the rebuild already? Emotion clogged my throat.

Sawyer zipped inside the school parking lot, avoiding chunks of asphalt and cracked concrete and pulled right onto the burnt lawn, stopping in front of a brand-new building. It was huge, two stories high and there were tradesmen installing doors and windows on the red brick building.

Red brick.

It looked like it was taken out of Paladin Village right down to the freshly planted garden beds. It was the only complete building on campus so far, but the others were going up quickly from the looks of it. Yet from what I could see of the materials, they were going to be glass and steel, the usual modern Werewolf City vibe.

"Sawyer?" I parked the bike and turned it off, glancing back to see Creek still asleep.

Sawyer stepped off his scooter and walked over to a lit up sign which had a piece of canvas draped over it. Reaching up, he ripped it off and I stared at the words etched into metal.

Paladin Cultural Studies Building

A sob left my throat as the realization of what this was settled into me.

"I thought Rab and Arrow could teach some classes here. And any of the Paladin that want to go to school here can too, but I think most importantly future city wolves need to learn more about our nature loving brethren." Sawyer said.

I laughed, wiping at my eyes and threw myself into his arms. "It's perfect."

He had no idea, did he? He had no idea that he was everything I never knew I needed. The glue to all the broken pieces inside of me. My wolf practically purred inside my chest at that, and I leaned forward, capturing Sawyer's mouth in a passionate kiss. When I pulled back, he was looking at me with half-lidded, bedroom eyes.

"You're stuck with me for life now, you know that, right?" I held up my ring finger and Sawyer's eyes crinkled at the edges as he smiled.

"Lucky me."

Life wouldn't be easy. We'd still have challenges running a pack with two alphas and two territories. I still had power-boosting blood that someone might one day want. But we were going to make the best of this amazing life we had, and create a beautiful future together with our son.

Forever.

THE END

CHAPTER 1

MY MOTHER PUSHED OPEN THE DOOR TO MY bedroom, allowing the light to leak inside. It took a second for my eyes to adjust to the sudden brightness, and when they did, her troubled face came into view. I'd been sitting in my dark room all day, avoiding the inevitable.

"It's time," she announced with resignation.

My gaze swept over the hard lines around her eyes—from years of worrying—then at her tearstained cheeks, but what stood out most of all was the red crescent moon tattoo on her forehead.

The symbol of a demon's slave. The symbol of my future.

Nodding, I lifted myself off my bed, with heavy limbs, and an even heavier heart. My mother stepped to the side as I passed her, and I made my way out into the living room.

Mikey, my younger brother, sat on the couch, staring at the smooth plaster walls as if by his sheer will, he could change the present. Nothing could change what I was about to do, what I was about to become. My fate had been written a long time ago.

"I wish I was the firstborn," my little brother muttered in a hollow voice that made my throat pinch with emotion. My normally goofball brother was near tears, and it *killed* me.

I didn't wish he were born first. I was glad it was me. My brother was too soft emotionally to live the life of a demon's slave. It was better this way.

"Today I wish I never had children," my mother said gravely.

I knew she didn't mean it. She just wanted to protect me from this, and wishing me out of existence would do that. That's how bad times were. Since The Falling, none of us had any hope at a normal life anymore; all we could do was wish things were different or accept what was.

My mother wiped her leaking eyes and straightened. "Maybe you'll get Necromancy like me and get a more prominent post. Then we could work together after your academy studies." Her mood instantly brightened at the thought.

I nodded, although it was highly unlikely. When the angels fell from Heaven and warred on Earth with Lucifer and his demons, powers flared out like the aurora borealis, infecting most of humanity. The Falling turned most of us into some sort of supernatural creature and left the rest human. Your gift depended on whether an angel or demon's power touched you during the fight. It was completely random and had nothing to do with whether or not you were a good person. My mother was demon gifted with Necromancy, and reanimated the dead for a living. It was the only reason we weren't living on the streets, like half of the human population. But they weren't really alive; the... things she reanimated were akin to zombies. I shuddered, thinking of the times she'd brought her work home with her.

"It won't be Necro, Mom. It's random. She could be a Gristle for all we know." There was my sarcastic Mikey, back in action.

My mom reached back and swatted his head. "Just be quiet," she chided. Her normally vibrant blond hair was dull and greasy. She'd no doubt stayed up all night worrying about this.

I laughed dryly to lighten the mood. If I was a Gristle, that would actually be the perfect shitty topping to my already shitty life. It meant having the magical ability to make trash disappear. Gristles smelled like crap, literally, and they were the bottom of the barrel as far as magical society class was concerned.

I was five years old when The Falling happened. My mom said that when the magic hit me, my body hovered in the air for a full five minutes, and she had to pin me to the bed to keep me from floating away. Mikey was four, so he wouldn't really remember, but she mentioned his skin had turned green for over an hour.

Stepping closer, my mother smoothed my bright blond hair down. "I'm sorry. I should never have taken the deal wi—"

I cut her off with a wave of my hand. Quite frankly, I was sick of the apology. My dad had been dying of cancer, and the whole family agreed that my mom would sell her services to the demons, becoming a lifelong Necro for the baddies. We just hadn't read the fine print, which stated your firstborn was also a lifelong slave to the wicked.

I'd have been fine with it, if my father hadn't been hit by a bus six months after the demons took his cancer. *Six months* of extended life was all that my mother's and my lifetime enslavement earned him. Life was jacked up, and I'd learned not to depend on sunshine and rainbows. The unicorns of my childhood dreams were dead and slaughtered.

Now summer was over and I was eighteen. Today I would go to The Awakening, a magical ceremony put on by the fallen angels to fully ignite our powers, to reveal what gifts or curses we held. Angel blessed or demon gifted—at least for those of us who had them. When The Falling first happened and all of the powers were unleashed on the humans, no one was sure who got hit or with what. When the angels realized what they'd done—mutated humanity—they contained all of the powers given to anyone under the age of eighteen. They couldn't take them back, but they could keep them at bay so we could have a childhood, at least.

Once my power was determined, I would exit stage left, get my demon slave tattoo, and enroll in the notoriously dysfunctional and scary Tainted Academy while the others exited stage right and enrolled in the Fallen Academy with the rest of the free souls. Fallen Academy was an exclusive college for those who weren't demon-slave bound, mostly the angel blessed. The supernaturally gifted would be trained for four years, and then be drafted into the Fallen Army, receiving good payment for their service to the light. We were still at war, after all, and I was about to sign up for the wrong side. My lifetime service to the demons would start today, and I felt sick thinking about it.

"I should get going. I don't want to be late," I said abruptly. That would result in my entire family being slaughtered by demons. They were greedily awaiting their new slave, a fresh eighteen-year-old to torture and wear down over the rest of my life.

My mom fell into a puddle of tears then and I just couldn't deal with it. I needed to stay strong or I was going to lose it.

"Love you guys. See you after," I added, ignoring my mother's weeping as I walked hastily to where my coat was hanging by the door.

"Brielle." My mother's voice carried so much emotion that I knew I wouldn't be able to turn around or I would completely fall to pieces. "I'm so sorry. Forgive me?"

The apology was old, but this was new. Did she think I blamed her? We'd all agreed that the healer demon we went to had tricked her. She had no idea a blood oath included her firstborn. I was twelve years old and mature enough to know what I had encouraged her to do. We all did it for my father.

That time I did turn around.

"Of course I forgive you, Mom. It's the demon scum that will never get my forgiveness." I hated them. Rage built in my chest as I grieved for my future. The future I would've had if they hadn't tricked my mother into giving up my life to save my father's. If he'd still been alive, it would've been worth it, but six months? It wasn't enough.

My mom just stood there and nodded. "Your father would—" She couldn't finish as the sob escaped her throat. I needed to get the hell out of there. It was too sad.

When the bus hit my father six years ago, I'd begged my mom to reanimate him so I could talk to him, tell him how much I loved him, and get bear hugs from him again. She refused, and at the time I'd hated her for it. As I grew older and interacted with the reanimated more, I understood why. They were zombies, shells of their former selves. Besides, he'd made her promise that she never would.

Suddenly, my mother and brother were both bearing down on me, arms around me, squeezing tight. "Maybe you'll be a dud and useless to everyone," my brother mumbled into my hair, and then we all broke apart laughing.

I punched his arm lightly. "There's only room for one dud in this family, and you've taken to that position beautifully." He just grinned and shook his head.

A dud was a nonmagical being. A human. They were rare in Los Angeles, since The Falling started there, but it did happen. Maybe I *would* be a dud, but I was sure the demons could find use for a human, and I was also sure my brother had magical abilities as well. That night of The Falling, when I was floating up in the air above my bed, I had a vivid memory of my brother lighting up like a Christmas tree, bright green.

Neither of us would be duds.

After that night, adults' gifts started showing immediately, but our gifts had to be locked down. Could you imagine a five-year-old Gristle eating up trash on the street? At least that part had been fair. We'd been given somewhat normal childhoods—if growing up with demons and fallen angels roaming the streets was normal. At least we weren't being made to raise the dead at seven years old.

"I love you guys. Everything's going to be fine," I reassured my family, with as much strength in my voice as I could muster.

A heavy sigh escaped my mom, and she reached out to touch my cheek. "You're wise beyond your years."

My throat tightened as unshed tears lined my eyes. My father used to say that to me. In fact, they were the last words he shared before he left for work and was taken from us.

ACKNOWLEDGMENTS

Big round of thanks to my editor, proofer, ARC team, PA's, Wolf Pack, designer, and the entire crew that is involved in releasing one of my books. I literally couldn't do this without you! A huge thank-you to the team at Bloom Books for publishing this series and getting it in stores. And finally, thank you to my family, who always shares me with my books because my characters don't seem to shut up. Love you mucho!

ABOUT THE AUTHOR

Leia Stone is the *USA Today* bestselling author of multiple bestselling series, including Matefinder, Wolf Girl, The Gilded City, Fallen Academy, and Kings of Avalier. She's sold over three million books, and her Fallen Academy series has been optioned for film. Her novels have been translated into multiple languages and she even dabbles in script writing.

Leia writes urban fantasy and paranormal romance with sassy kick-butt heroines and irresistible love interests. She lives in Spokane, Washington, with her husband and two children.

Instagram: @leiastoneauthor
TikTok: @leiastone
Facebook: leia.stone
Website: www.LeiaStone.com